CURB FEELER

BY: J.C. COLLERY

Columbus, Ohio

This book is a work of fiction. The names, characters and events in this book are the products of the author's imagination or are used fictitiously. Any similarity to real persons living or dead is coincidental and not intended by the author.

The views and opinions expressed in this book are solely those of the author and do not reflect the views or opinions of Gatekeeper Press. Gatekeeper Press is not to be held responsible for and expressly disclaims responsibility of the content herein.

Curb Feeler

Published by Gatekeeper Press
2167 Stringtown Rd, Suite 109
Columbus, OH 43123-2989
www.GatekeeperPress.com

Copyright © 2021 by J.C. Collery
All rights reserved. Neither this book, nor any parts within it may be sold or reproduced in any form or by any electronic or mechanical means, including information storage and retrieval systems, without permission in writing from the author. The only exception is by a reviewer, who may quote short excerpts in a review.

The cover design and editorial work for this book are entirely the product of the author. Gatekeeper Press did not participate in and is not responsible for any aspect of these elements.

ISBN (paperback): 9781662915888
eISBN: 9781662915895

This story, as vulgar and unconventional as it may be, was only possible with the constant encouragement of my biggest fan and critic.
My biggest inspiration to write.
Heres to you, Mom.
-J.C.

"There he sat, pondering his next move, as if he had one. The way the world was turning had its effect on him and he fell off."

This all started about a week ago, or so he thought. His extent of frustration had peaked and one could say he has lost control. Not to say that a very fiery downward spiral did not lead to this point, but it appears he has finally crashed into the ocean. Extinguishing the flames, and burning out. Which he decided was the better option than fading away.

* * * * * * * * * * * * * * * * * * *

He is the product of an unfortunate fortune. There was a time when this boy was happy, unfortunately those days are over. Now he resorts to the pseudo happiness that various chemicals award him. It's hard to tell where it all started.
Maybe back in the day.

He sat helpless in a noisy, dirty room most of his early life. Polluted with loud, children's music that was intended to drown the constant shouting that prevailed from his single mother's neighboring room. His best friend, a stuffed koala bear toy that an unknown man gave him, a relic of an unknown father that his mother never knew. She decided to leave her four-year-old son at the park bathrooms one afternoon, maybe a sign that she was ready to go. She was found dead about a week later. Unfortunately, she died from a heroin overdose while riding the bus one afternoon. The driver found her after doing nearly two full routes. When the bus driver noticed, he got a little angry and was shouting at her to wake up. By that time she was cooked.

He was found shortly after she left him. A man riding a bike found him crying near the soda machines. The police were not sure what to do with the boy so he ended up being in adoptive care for many years. After some time, he was adopted at the age of sixteen. They were nice people though, an older Jewish man and his wife, as wise as a couple could be. They raised him from that point forward. Caring for everything he needed, and agreeing to never tell him of his true mothers past or location. It hardly mattered though, as he found out shortly after being adopted and decided to rebel by eating all his adoptive fathers blood pressure medication. That was the first time he got high, for about fifteen minutes and then collapsed on the mantle and broke some of his new mothers trinkets and keepsakes. Causing a ruckus before laying his head into the edge of a door. His mother was less than thrilled. Shortly after being released from the hospital for that suicide attempt, he dived headfirst into a bottle of codeine based painkillers and a bottle of Jim Beam.

A hallucination of swimming, and the water is ice cold. A vast, empty underwater wasteland that he is so scared, yet so comfortable to be in. He cannot breath and he simply doesn't care. The water is dark, yet he begins to tread forward in an attempt to find something. His jagged, tense movements in an environment of absolute zero. He looks around, before quickly making an attempt forward and feels a cold object at his fingertips. He directs at that feeling and gets two hands on it. It feels like two arms. He can tell it's human. The cold flesh is wrapped in what feels like the sleeve of a loose fitting, lightweight, feminine garment. He struggles as he cannot see in this pitch black. He screams, but no words are audible. A pain in his chest stabs through him as he is ripped into a dark hole. Grasped to life on a gurney in the emergency room.

     A teenage boy. Comfortable with the thought of death. In fact, he feels he would *rather* be dead.

     It was at this point that his parents took a step back for a while, and the state decided he needed professional help. So, at the late age of seventeen he was involuntarily admitted to a program for adolescents at risk. He stayed 10 long months in that place before he left on his eighteenth birthday. His living with equally disturbed or impacted youth had given him the know how that he needed to safely, yet effectively numb himself and get him closer to what he has always wanted. An end to all the pain, and an easier way of living.

     The struggles he faced made him tough. Naturally, he was incredibly persuasive. A real terror to any nervous father. A sociopath with good work ethic. Never afraid to take it to the limits just to get what he wanted. So, in such a delicate world, he thrived.

     He first took a job some years after his 21st birthday as a sales representative for a small technology company. At the time, they were selling the pager. An amazing invention that only needed to be introduced before it could sell itself. He was an excellent salesmen. So capable of finding a marriage of interest between product and customer that he immediately excelled as a salesman. He made his first bit of money and kept it saved. Living like a grease ball, he sold dozens of pagers a day, racking up large amounts of cash in short periods of time and stock piling the proceeds. Being as cheap as one could be and free of any type of temptation. He marvels in himself. He developed a real obsession with his own image. He would check his looks in the dirty bathroom of a cheap apartment before his sales job. Eventually, he is noticed for his consistence in excellence and is offered a better position. To which he welcomes with gratitude. Left in his wake, a slurry of happy customers and angry coworkers that would eventually lose their jobs to his outstanding people skills. He breaks free of modern conflict. Carrying your tongue for you while you throw it in cuss. Before he snaps it out, and steps on your ego. Most conflict is left in his favor.

     Women fall for him left and right and he cares little of their affection. He never felt the love of a women in any conventional way. An object of their affection, a whisper in their ear. He shook off the affection of humans with an overtly found reclamation for his own self loathing. He felt warmer this way.

In all, we can decipher that he was a "somebody" once upon a time. But now? Just a common everyday street rat. He can wake in his everyday squalor in an almost bittersweet content. He finds some feeling of relief in the fact that he is not a part of the everyday hustle and bustle that the world had come to be. He has a strong dislike of the common man now. An introvert, with a hint of hatred and disgust. He could bare the modern man in an almost humorous fashion. Mocking their modern day intellect with his old fashioned wits. An old soul of sorts. He captures his fill of all the modern day hustle and bustle, and finally has snapped. He sees no love, no affection, no honest pain. He misses his youth, a failure to surrender the tendencies of his younger day. He finds his new found life hard. A perfect contradiction. The feeling of being stranded fills his everyday life.

This is the story of his final peak. His perpetual, mired passage to the physical world before he checked out.

We join this man as he awakes in his shanty, a true expression of his energy.

* * * * * * * * * * * * * * * * * * * *

Brucie.

I woke up on the floor of the basement apartment that I am squatting in. A little bit of daylight penetrating the improvised cardboard box window blinds is burning my brain. Made worse by the assortment of various street drugs that were present in my system from the night before. I scoop myself off the dirty floor like the freshly dumped, steaming pile of shit that I am. Shit, or at least what I feel like.

"Aw.. Fuckin' sweet!"

I am enthused upon the discovery of a slurry of cigarette butts from the night before. This is necessary so I can salvage the innards to roll another smoke from the tobacco left in the butts.

A knock sounds from the door, and as always. Perfect timing.

"Fuck!" I say as I scurry a bit in fear. As it may be the homeowner coming to kick me out again.

"Come in!"

It's Larry.

"What's up Brucie?" He asks.

Before I continue, I should take a moment to introduce Larry, or more importantly Scary Larry. Larry, is short for Larry Beatsmen, or Larry S. Beatsmen, as if anyone needed to know. Anyway, he earned the name "Scary Larry" on account of the effect that various drugs have on him. It didn't matter if he was drinking beer or brief casing cocaine, the guy is a fucking mess when he gets ripped.

"You wanna' split that?" he asks, as I knew he would.

"Yeah, I guess." I answer. I mean after all, I know this isn't the best cigarette, but he is staring at it like its a damn crack pipe. Gets a man thinking.

"Hey Lar- you got anything?"

"Not really man," He answers "I got this roach. It's poo-poo, but it'll give you a pretty decent-"

I cut him off.

"Let me see it!"

I grab the little brown joint roach from his hand. It smells like the secret pocket of Larry's two month unwashed, dumpster jeans.

"Fuck it, grab the can."

I break up the concentrated poo-poo clip and put the salty remains on the crevice of my pipe that is fashioned from an old beer can.

"Where's your flame?" I ask.

"I don't have one." Larry answers.

I am about to fucking lose it. Maybe it is the thought of not being able to smoke my fine Turkish-domestic menthol-blend class E cigarette, but damn. What did I do to deserve this? Larry and I proceed to tear the spot apart looking for any damn object that could possibly hold a flame. We find one match. With no striker. I'm feeling a little slap happy at this point. Some life. I go from being a king, well, at least in *my world,* to this. I cannot even light my damn smoke. We finally manage to light the cigarette off the toaster, which is dumb because I wanted to save the cigarette until after we were lit, but whatever. Beggar's can't be choosers.

    I sit down next to Larry and spark the match off the cherry of the makeshift cigarette. Larry looking at me with that fucking face. I want to tear that fucking thing off that stupid head sometimes. Such a schmuck. I pass him the can.

    "Don't chief it man!" I say with a breathy lung full of rotten smoke. No coughing here.

    "Ugh! That shit taste like a mix between asshole and beer!"

    The roach only gave up three hits, but I got two, so I am feeling a little relieved. What is happening in my gut though, feels disastrous. I have to go. Nowhere in particular, I mean I have to "go," and by how intense this is feeling, there is no way I am making it to the get-go mart. I sit here faced with a huge dilemma. See, I am what is called a "squatter." This means I am staying illegally at a domicile. This translates roughly to no running water, no electricity, no toilet, no toilet paper, no modern appliances, nothing. Well, with the exception of a toaster oven and microwave that Larry and I got out the garbage a few months back. So, now we get to the source of power for these fine pieces of modern day luxury. That dilemma was remedied via a dark green extension cord I had laying around from my early days. We found an outdoor outlet near the power drop down on the neighbors house. It's a little short, so to use it you have to put the appliance in front of the door with the cord going out the door jam. Yes, this is illegal, so we try not to use it, or even be in the spot when the neighbors were around. The last thing I need is some cop giving me shit for the things I have to do to survive.

    My gut starts humming.

    "Oh shit. I gotta' take a dump, man!" I proclaim.

    Larry laughs.

    "That's *toooo* bad man!"

    He really knows how to piss me off. But, no worse than the ever so important fact that I am at a lack of toilet paper. I started ripping around the spot. Ended up finding an old sock. So I head out to do my business. Problem solved. I drop that hot evil next to a telephone poll behind some shrubs on the street, and head back to the basement.

"I seal team six'd that shit, bro!" I say with relief.
Larry chuckles.

It's good to make people happy again. Even if it's a joke about bowel movement. Even if it makes me sad later. I enjoy making someone laugh, it doesn't matter if it's on, or at me. I'm past that point. My life is the prime example of karma, and if they are laughing to hurt me, it will come back on them. I understand that now.

"I'm hungry" I say, yawning in between saying it so I had to repeat myself. I hate that.

Anyway, I have some cereal left from that bag of Sweetie-O's. No milk, so I eat it dry. My mouth feels like I've been chewing fiberglass insulation. I haven't brushed my teeth in at least two weeks, and when I do, I have to use the water fountain at the park. It's a little salty but it works. I like to assume I'm decently healthy though. Even though it's probably horribly untrue.

I am feeling rather stimulated. The Sweetie-O's must be kicking in. With this burst of energy, priority comes to mind. I grab the pen and pad that I keep under the old porno magazines that Larry found in the dumpster behind the get-go mart, and start to compile a list:

Do pick up list.
A breakdown of what needs to happen.

- Steal napkins from get-go mart.
- Steal toilet paper from port-o-pooper. (check park bathrooms)
- Get cups from any restaurant
- Get some $ together, get won tons. GET SAUCE (it helps with cereal)
- Find a god damn cigarette!
- Get a lighter (or a match)
- Ditch Larry, try to get smoked up
- Try to peddle some poo-poo
- Find some poo-poo
- Get a ride to the mall (Found $5 there)
- Get a job for the day.
- Find a party
- Steal a loaf of bread, a toothbrush, a bucket, a bar of soap. Just steal anything.
- Steal eggs.
- Steal beer.
- Buy beer for minors (Don't come back this time!)

This is my list of things I would like to accomplishing today. It may or may not be completed, but I will sleep at the end of the day.

I snap back to consciousness to see Larry writing something on an old liquor receipt.

"What the fuck are you doing Larry?" I ask.

"What the fuck you think I'm doin? I'm writin'! I'm educated you know?"

He gives me that fucking look again.

"Gimme' that!" I snatch the receipt from his hand.

"HEY! Whatta' ya'-"

"Shut up Larry!" I interject.

I look at the receipt, it has five crude letters thrown together and poorly written on it:

"C M N D R"

I have to pause for a moment to try and understand it.

"What, the fuck Larry! Stop doing drugs you fucking dumb ass!" I shout.

He starts to get red, really red. That fucking face, it is in full effect.

"Larry... Stop fucking looking at me man!"

He is really looking like he is going to swing at me. It's not a big deal because he is a sack of shit and I will put his damn face in the toaster. I remember once Larry picked a fight with some senior citizen biker dude at a picnic in the park. The dude mopped the floor with Larry. I have to say, even as a friend, it was funny to see Larry try to pick a fight with the biker.

For those who don't know him, the best way to describe Larry is a five foot, five inch tall, meatball of a man. I think he said he weighed 190 pounds. Not an ounce of muscle on him. A pale, red, sweaty man with a weight problem. I'm assuming it is just his persona considering he has been homeless forever and must have been genetic because his dad was a big guy too. Larry talked about his dad pretty often. Talking about the "good old days." I can't imagine how good they were. Larry's dad died early, and in a humorous, yet unfortunate sequence of events.

Larry's dad choked, on an apple core. See Larry has always been broke. His dad, died because he was picking the dumpsters at the elementary school. I'll explain, one day, the cops pulled up and started to run for them. Larry always described that dumpster as a "fuckin' buffet." Anyway, Larry's old man started running. He loaded his pockets with expired milk cartons and grabbed the apple core of his eye. He hopped out of the dumpster with the apple core in his mouth. Larry's dad forgot to tuck and roll and got that apple core so lodged down his throat, I think they buried him with it in. Hell of an after party. Funny thing about it is, to this day, Larry is terrified of apple cores. I guess that's a good thing though, I hear the apple doesn't fall far from the tree.

"*YO!*" Larry rolls up off the dumpster couch.

"What do you want man, you trying to start some shit here, Scary Larry!?" I respond in an antagonizing tone. He looks like he is going to pop.

"Don't *you* make fun of me… you… you… fucking *WASH OUT!*" Larry cries.

I assume he meant "wash up." Like I am a washed up nobody. But with Scary Larry, there is no knowing. For all I know, he meant wash out. Which in his mind has a whole another meaning.

"Wash out!?" I scream at him.

"Yeah, a wash out!" He responds.

He had that stupid face on him. I am speechless, bug then I spoke.

"Larry. First of all, it's fucking washed up you dumb son of a bitch, and second of all, don't ever call me that again or I will seriously rip your damn throat out!"

By then, he calmed down. I thought he might be having a heart attack.

"Okay man, I'm cool, I am sorry Brucie." He says.

"It's alright man, I'm sorry too." I respond.

"Come on, I'm gonna' be late." I say as if I had somewhere important to go, or anything to do at all.

Larry jumped like I said I had a bag of cookies and we were going to that dumpster at the school. I also caught a waft of him when stood up and I swore he shit his pants, or at least it smelled like he did.

"Larry, put that fuckin' face away, man." I laugh with him.

* *

We venture out of the smelly dungeon I call home with no money in our pockets and a fuzzy headache of a buzz that the poo-poo had given us.

"So where are we going?" Larry asks.

"Oh.. Larry, I forgot to tell you! You have to get lost for a bit, I am gonna' go do some shit." I answer.

He muddles back with a nervous; "What?" before I can see the rage begin to build.

I could tell because he is making that face again. I couldn't *actually* bring him though. I just need him out of that place when I am not there.

"Yeah dude, big plans. Larry, you gotta' hit the old dusty trail. Kick rocks."

He looks like he is about to cry.

"Fine!" He whimpers.

Larry stormed off like an Irish man walks away from the bottle. I knew he would be knocking on my door as soon as possible.

I walk onto Smea Street, broke and without Larry. This is the hot spot of Smog Town. Whatever you need you could get here. Except barbecue. Which sucks because I like barbecue. I walk east, down Smea Street, headed towards a small convenience store turned gas station that has a wide variety of items and minimal security. I would usually come here to scratch a few things off my list or use the bathroom. I blast the door open like I own the place, maybe a little too hard because I knocked a cardboard display onto a middle aged women. She looks familiar, but is just very angry and stomped off too quickly for me to make out her features any further. I then locked eyes with the store clerk.

"Yo Brucie!" He yells.

The two kids that work at the store at night are identical twins. This really fucked with me for the first couple months after they were hired because they would work the same shift, and I would think the clerk is some sort of teleporting magician. After a couple inebriated confrontations with the boys I got to know them and found out that their uncle was actually the owner of the store. It wasn't long before I was buying them bottles of beer from the store and leaving them next to the dumpsters out back. Ever since then we kind of had an agreement. They don't snitch on me, I won't snitch on them. Of course, the ball is really in their court. But they are just too dumb to realize it.

"Oh shit! What's good Chester?"

Chester, and his, presently absent brother Marcus were the guy's behind the counter. They were tall, lanky, and kind of goofy. I think they were from India or at least their family was. These two are strange. Their voices high pitched and their glasses thick. They do keep the store pretty clean. They are alright, plus they let me steal stuff. Sometimes they would come through with some good smoke. None of those poo-poo fuzziness squat nuggets.

"Hey man, did you hear about Brian?" Chester asks. I have no idea who Brian was or what the hell he is talking about.

"Yeah man, it sucks." I replied. I do this to avoid any prolonged conversations with this giant of a little boy.

"Yeah. Too young man. Too young." Chester adds.

I don't truly mind having a conversation with Chester. He had an alright personality. The dude's vision though, it is fucking shot. He always thought someone was out to get him as well. So he would spend most of the conversation looking at his busted car, squinting, and not paying attention to what I was shoving into my jacket pockets. That reminds me.

"Hey Chester, when do you get off?" I ask.

"Hmm, like three and a half hours." He responds, taking his cell phone out of his pocket and bringing it very close to his face to check the time.

"Oh, that sucks. Hey, do you have a cig' I can bum?"

I hate bumming cigarettes. It is a stupid burden to me and I hated having to ask for things. Even if it was a bogie. I guess that's why the term 'bumming' bothered me as well.

"Yeah I got you. Hell, it is the least I can do for a local lush an all!"

Damn it. He went there. He reaches under the counter and pulls out a pack of some cheap brand menthol cigarettes. What a waste of money. He reaches in the pack and pulls two out and hands them to me. By then, there is a line forming and my pockets were about to burst.

"Got a pack of matches?" I ask with a nervous grin.

He slaps down a pack of matches on the counter. We're in business.

I walk outside with a grocery bag full of crap and two cigarettes. I am on top of the world. I have been in town for all of about 10 minutes, and am already killing it. I head back to the place I call home to unload my goodies. The town is coming alive a bit as I am heading back. About a quarter mile away from the gas station a car drove by full of drunken young women, one of them yelling out the window:

"I'll suck your dick!"

It wasn't even night time, and these girls are already drunk enough to yell this type of thing at a clearly homeless looking man on the street. A few moments later I arrive at 'home' and gently budge the door open. Once inside, I decide to assess the spoils of my recent adventure:

- Three packs of snack cakes.
- Handful of napkins.
- 1 Pack of hot dogs.
- 2 loose beers.
- A bundle of plastic utensils.
- 4 ketchup packets.
- 1 Pack of gum.
- 2 cigarettes.
- 1 pack of matches.
- 1 chocolate bar.

I pull one of the cigarettes from my ear and strike up a match. The cheap menthol burns my mouth and nose. That combined with the taste of an early match makes the taste absolutely terrible. It did not matter though. I smoke poo-poo roaches out of an old moldy beer can. This is a *treat* compared to that. I pull the cigarette slow, to prevent it from hot boxing. I reach over to my stockpile and grab the candy bar I had stolen. It is half way melted. One hell of a meal. It reminds me back to a time a few years ago when I was a little bit more successful. This one particular time when I walked into a Smog Town store to pay for gas or some shit and I ended up buying a couple packs of cigarettes and a candy bar. I didn't know why the hell I always bought candy bars. It must have been some childhood thing. Then it manifests to stealing them. That makes sense. See I was a kid once, a pretty happy kid given the circumstances. But once I was actually adopted, I did *love* my adoptive family in a way. But I am sure they didn't love me the same. I actually know Smog Town because it was a little bit north of where my family lived and we would go there often. We would do all types of fun shit. My adoptive dad. He was a good father, very loving and caring. Anyway the point here is that way back when I was a teenager we used to go into stores or gas stations, and I would steal. He never approved of it but he never told me to bring it back. I guess he just cared too much to make me feel bad in an overwhelming way. This didn't mean he would not punish me, but he was more interested in my power to 'stick it to the man.' I remember him saying how the companies would not really suffer. He explained mark up, profit, source, and distribution. It all made sense. So you could say I learned quick, but also developed a habit. Anyway, back to my story. I was in the store and bought all this crap, pointlessly I might add. There was this homeless guy just outside the door. He was asking for spare change, or probably what ever you would give him, and I debated just giving him the candy. I didn't even eat the fucking chocolate bar. It melted in my glove box and got all over my registration and a gold watch I had. Where is that watch now? Shit, with the car I'm guessing. I'm an idiot. I'm pretty sure there was a pack of cigarettes in there too.

    I open the melted chocolate bar and squeeze the hot contents into my mouth. It is a lot like eating shit. Shit with a hint of cheap breath mints. Combine that with my dry mouth and halitosis and it is a combo better than hard liquor and a smoke. Then came a knock on the door.

    "Who is it?" I shout.

    A muffled voice responds:

    "It's Slappy Lobsta', son!"

    The "Slappy Lobster" as he is trying to pronounce, is probably one of the coolest people you could ever meet. A chubby Jamaican man with poor grammar and endless wit. He smokes his weight in ganja every day and is always looking to talk something about "ital" or "blood clot" or something. I never fully understood him but I always know what he is saying.

    "Holy shit man! What's good?" I ask as I greet him at the door.

    "Na' too much ya' Brucie. How yas' been?"

    I paused for a second to put it all together.

"Not too bad Slappy, I'm just sittin' here. Eating some shit."
I raised my hand containing the melted chocolate bar.

"Ya' I see's dat'! It smells lik' Larry's blood clot ass was 'ere. Tat' rassclat fool been holdin' me' up on a twinty' fi' dollah's Brucey!"

I start laughing about three quarters of the way through his ramble and respond:

"You're not gonna' get your money, man. I'm telling you. Larry just won't do it."

Slappy shakes his head and continues:

"Ah' shit mane. Tat' fuckin' guy! Wat' a pile ove' shit! Pitiful blood clot comes round reeking like a rotten beer. Talkin' all type of shit. I was bout' to roll up on tat' fool!"

He sparks up a joint of some real funky smelling, dry, crackly weed. He takes a puff and breaks from his rant. He continues with a lung full of smoke as he speaks, giving him a much more deep tone.

"Motha' Fucka' walks into me mom's joint. Talkin' som'tin 'bout som' guy who almost hit him wile' he was crossin' the road, down there round park street. Larry stat' talkin' all type a mess bout' how he wood smack' dat' man if he could. I laugh at de' fool. tell him right there' tat' he should shut tha' fuck up and close da' door! Motha' fucka' jus' stand there' givin' me this' dumb fuckin' look tat' blood clot be makin'. So what da' motha' fucka' do? He just stand' there and ask me if I can get em' som' weed! I tell em' dunce bat I no sell tis sheet just like every otta' time he come round askin'. Then he jus' start bitchin' tell me make' the call'. Bong belly pickney, aint' got' no dolla's anyway!"

I respond by shaking my head, and saying:
"Sounds like Larry to me!"

Slappy passes the joint to me. I hit it. Inhale, and pass it back. I notice that there is a little bit of chocolate on the end of the joint.

"Shit man, sorry! I am out of toilet paper and-" I say jokingly.

Slappy drops the joint and the mood changes for the worse.

"AY' OH! Wat' da' fuck is tat'!" He yells.

"Dude, I said I was sorry!" I respond smiling, as if he knows I am joking. His face tells a story of heartbreak and disgust.

"Mon' tat' so fucking gross'! How can you jus sit deh covered eena sheet'? Wah' di fuck!?"

I guess I should now to tell him the joke.

"Chill Slappy! It's fuckin' chocolate, man! Relax!"

Needless to say, it didn't calm him down.

His accent and Patois language was really coming out now.

"Dont yuh jus bi a tell mi tuh relax yuh ah fucking mess mon. Wah mek nuh yuh git yuh shit togedda yuh fucking loser!"

I am just sitting here dreaming of punching Slappy's face in, but who am I kidding. He is right. He is completely right. My pride escapes me and I crumble like an ant hill in the rain.

"I'm sorry." I mumble. Just loud enough to even make it heard. In an attempt to see if he will even notice.

"Nah!" he responds. "Mi nuh fucking wid yuh nuh muh Brucie. Fucking do someting' mon. Yuh such ah pile ah shit. All yuh evah duh a waak yuh batty roun dis town stealing fram di stores and shit."

I am stunned. Chills run up and down my body. That was cold, real cold. Slappy could rip you up. He is just too honest. Honest to the point where if he is insulting you, you were sure he wasn't just being mean, but he was being serious. I must have really pissed him off. I felt my nose start to sting. A tell tale sign that I was about to tear up. He went on talking.

"Mi nuh believe it. mi a sidung here, smoking yuh up pan dis an yuh cova fi mi smoke all up wid chocol mon. Yuh ah fucking joke mon!"

"STOP! Just stop!" I yell.

"Look! I'm sorry bro! I'm fucking sorry about the joint. Dude, you gotta' get the hell out of here Slappy. Thanks for smoking me up, but you gotta' get the hell out of here!"

"Fuck you!" He responds.

He sat up, stomps for the door, and swings it open. He looks at me one more time and shook his head. Then slammed the door shut. I could feel that helpless self pity that one might feel. Almost like I was about to blat.

"What an asshole." I say.

I have to get out of here. I head for the door but as soon as I touch the knob, Larry knocks. I know it is him because of his four knock method that he always uses. I open the door.

"What's up Brucie? You alright?" Larry asks.

"Yeah, I'm cool man, what's up?" I answer.

Larry went on.

"Nothin' man. What are you doing?"

"I'm just chilling man. Slappy was just here and I got melted chocolate all over a joint we were smoking and he kinda' freaked out." I say.

Larry lights up with excitement.

"Yeah! I just saw him leave! He shoved me at the door!" Larry says this like he is excited to have it done to him.

I shake my head in an almost elliptical fashion. Unsure if I should agree or disagree.

"Yeah, it's messed up. Whatever though man. He just rolled through here, then gave me a bunch of shit because of it."

It is then that I realized that I had just smoked, so my eyes are all red. That meant Larry would not be able to tell I am about to blat like a baby.

"I'm about to get out of here, Larry." I say.

"Alright man, I'll come by later." Larry responds.

"No, don't." I rebut, sarcastically.

I round up the two beers from the bed. Opening one and putting the other in my front pocket. Also grabbing a pack of the snack cakes off the bed. Then made the decision to leave the spot I call home. I realize that I have nowhere to go. So I walk, sucking back the shitty beer and getting a decent buzz.

It is funny where "nowhere to go" will take you. It is usually the most obscure places on the planet, yet it's always so common. Your mind is a wonderful power plant. It is when the power is lost, that you lose control of what you're thinking. The mind never really shuts down, instead it is more prone to run free.

    I wander endlessly into the abyss that my mind has ultimately designed me to fall victim to. I swear I am only walking through town, not my memories. Do I turn back? I know that I want to, but is it time? I should just wander on. All of life is surrounding me now. In terms that it is constant. Life is so powerful. It has the power to submerge you in itself and shape you around to find whatever you might think "life" is. I remember a few years ago, how free I was. How much love I had around me, and how much love I had to give. Life was brilliant. It shadowed my excellence perfectly and made me so proud to be myself. I spent more time having fun and living my life, than struggling. Truthfully, that in my opinion, *was* a golden age. I can't believe how well off I was! I wasn't making a *ton* of money, but it was just so damn much compared to anything else in my life, it may have sidetracked me. Fuck the money! That was nothing! I had life, and control of it. I was set.

    That pinch in the side of my skull sets in. That coppery taste. I am getting stressed.

    God I miss her.

    The love of my life was there. It is amazing how great you can feel when you have someone to tell you that they love you. She is somewhere. She is not dead or anything. I just don't think she would want me. We broke each others hearts, a very rare occasion. It is the worst when you don't know if they still want you or not. I walked by a spot where we once kissed. I stopped. I take a deep breath and remembered my father. The shit that man had to go through in his life. Mind boggling.

    "Women." I say, mockingly.

    The walk continues. I stumble down the lonely path that I call "the night." Fifteen minutes must have past before I get to a point where I feel familiar. I run into some twenty-something year old kids near Old Town. They were playing some poorly composed music on the corner, and quite loudly I might add.

    "Hey, you dirty motherfuckers!" I yell at them. "Turn your fucking music down before I come over there and spank your ass like your mother never did!"

    The boys turn the knob on their amp to turn the music down. One of the boys stands up and gives me a squinted look, to which I respond with a scowl.

"Brucie!?" He shouts.

"What?!" I respond.

I take a closer look and notice that it is Dave. Dave is an old friend from a time when I was into micro dosing hallucinogens. I am not sure why this late twenties man is doing hanging out with kids that look like they were still in high school. But then again, we probably shouldn't have been hanging out with *him* back then either. Dave runs up to me and goes for a high five.

"Bruuucie!" He yells.

"What's up, Dave?" I ask.

"Oh, nothing man. I was just chillin' and watching the stars with these kids and then I caught a..."

I stopped listening and remembered how I met this weirdo. Now, I don't exactly remember all their names but I will make do. Now pay attention:

So Dave used to chill with Dean, who was dating Dana. But Dana was a major slut, so she was banging Dave and Dale at the same time. So Dean doesn't chill with Dave any more, but he sometimes still chills with Dale. Dave is still tight with Doug and Dale though. Doug's not banging anybody though because he thinks Dave is his boy, and he "don't play that' shit." But truthfully, Doug doesn't give a shit, and was banging Deal (who was a big girl) at the same time he was banging Dean's Dana! If Dave knew this he would be destroyed. Doug does chill with Dan though, who is tight with this kid Devon. Devon was getting with Dom, which is short for Dominique. This was disastrous because Doug is also getting with Dom! But Doug knows Devon through Dom, who just broke up with Don by the way. So there is a lot of drama there. So then, while this was all going on. Don, Dom's ex, was banging Doris. And Doris? Well she was banging Dale the whole time anyway! The whole situation was just fucked.

Anyway, I snap back to Dave saying something about Acid or LSD.

"Whoa! Hold up. You got some tabs?" I ask abruptly.

"Yeah boy! Why? You want a hit or two, only three bucks a pop!"

"I'm broke, man. I would, but I have nothing. Can you spot it?" I ask, as if I would end up paying him. Not a chance in hell he is getting paid for this.

"Yeah. You better pay me though, here!"

He drops two pieces of perforated paper on my hand and I eat them immediately, and gave him a fist bump before heading on my merry way.

I walk in an iniquitous fashion toward the water of Smog Town. A dirty, smelly collection of sea water the featured a shallow beach and larger parking lot. It is a hot night. A sense of deprivation in the air. It is thick with humidity. Almost like breathing Jell-O. It is disgusting, dirty, foul, malnourished, and invasive, but I love it. I sit by the water on a piece of damp sand near the water. My legs start to feel crisp, and energized. A slight tingling. A sure sign that the lysergic acid is starting to course through my veins. My body fights the vasoconstriction. I start to clench up. I start to feel fear, a sense of insecurity. I know if I don't relax I can send myself into a dark corner of my own mind, a place I surely don't want to be. The only compulsory thought I could conceive was: Run... Run!

I stand up and take a deep breath. A quick gander into the bay water. A feeling of relief.
I take off at full speed, or rather an unshapely run into a low tide pool of water. As it gains depth, I slow down and begin to swim. Disregarding the things in my pockets, or the clothes on my body. I stop to a point where I could float on my back freely. I can certainly feel the effects of the substance now. I feel great. An absolutely free spirit just floating along the water as if I am a part of it. I don't know how long I floated there. Time has taken a new form and was no longer an issue. How long will this last? How long can I feel this good and stay in this mentality? I hope, forever. But I'm sure, it won't be anywhere near that long.

It must have been at least an hour later before I wash gently onto the shore. Covered in sea foam and sea weed, stinking of low tide and fish feces. I walk staggeringly to the outdoor public showers just east of the spot I came ashore on. Sure enough, there is a group of teenagers sitting near the showers up to no good, plain and simple. I pause upon seeing them, it shocked me as I was still feeling the effects of the LSD. A sure sign of weakness on my part. It is funny really. No matter how advanced we become as a society, instinct never fails. Fuck it, I continue to the shower and hit the button on the wall to make the weak stream of water hit me on the head to try and clean off all the muck. I can hear the teenager's sneakers strike the ground as one of them jumps down from the adjacent roof. I turn around in animosity. The boy lock eyes with me and approach with bad intentions. He shouts over to his friends while approaching.

"How much has he seen?!"

The boys respond differently but to a common consensus of: "I don't know."

It must have been the acid but this whole thing was happening in slow motion in my head. I suppose it benefited me in retrospect.

The kid throws a punch at me. A strong jab. For some incredible reason, I duck it just in the perfect amount of time for him to miss my face and smash the brick shower wall behind me. I heard the bones *crunch*. I guess that was *his* sign of weakness. As I am ducking, I notice that the boy has a wrapped up item in his left hand. I glance at that and then realized that I was now supposed to defend myself. I shot up my whole body weight into one punch and connected right square underneath the kids jaw bone. I could hear the young mans jaw crack. He fell backward and landed on his back, gurgling in pain and clinging to consciousness. I act fast, and exploited his broken hand. I quickly jump over his leg and lay my foot directly on top of his hand, then spun around on it to face his three friends. The kid let out a truly spine tingling whine and finally passed out due to the pain. I look at the boys, all three of them, from left to right, making eye contact with each one. I then look at the ground in front of them and stomped again harder on the kid's broken hand. The three kids jumped back and left running. I guess I took out their alpha.

"Let's see what we have got here. You thought you were a thug, huh?"

I grab the wrapped package off of the boy. A number of rectangular blocks are inside. Surely, what feels like bricks of money. I start to feel my heart race in excitement, that feeling like I'm going to mess my pants. I knew it was time to be rushing back to my place, fueled by the thought of money and the LSD, I got there double fast. I threw some random stuff in front of the door to act as a barrier of sorts. Protection from a possible angry retribution. I drop the package on the floor and look at it before tearing it open.

Four stacks of cash: Two bundles of $10,000 in denomination of one-hundred dollar bills, a stack of $2000 in fifty-dollar bills, and $500 in twenties. Surely, drug money. My heart races, and now I really feel the urge to void my bowels. Twenty-two thousand and five hundred fucking dollars. Oh my goodness. The rest of that night comes to escape me.

* *

I awoke from an innocuous slumber with a notable headache. Unsure of the day or time. Heart tachycardia visual through the beaten, dirty, button up shirt that is loosely covering the sloppy navel of my malnourished gut. I clear my throat in dry agony and spit's the vial product across the horrible mess of a room I so confidently call the "bone yard." It is obvious I am suffering from detoxification trauma. I move my pseudo-rigor mortis body off of the dirty mattress and waddle to the makeshift dresser where a variety of mind altering substances are present. This is new.

I gander over the plethora of powders, pills, herbs, concentrates, and chemicals. All to their own respect with their own power. Twinkle in my eye.

"What the fuck?"

I am very confused as to what has happened, or how I acquired all this stuff.

"What will it be today?" I say, as it feels so unfamiliar to me.

I sprung to action with an analog response and shuffle through the plastic bag of unlabeled vials of various materials and colors. I eventually came across a clear dish containing a yellow-brown paste. I was hoping it was some sort of opiate. I load a finger with the paste and wrap my tongue around it. Then rub the paste all over my gums and teeth. A strange whimper in response to the awful taste, but strangely, it was satisfying. This is quickly followed by my nose plummeting into a small pile of what appeared to be left over cocaine that was scattered across a cracked piece of a mirror that I must have found in the trash last night. My "cup of coffee" so to speak.

Rocket ship.

I moan in discontent as I catch a glimpse of myself in the mirror. What happened last night? I remember the fight, and the acid, and of course the money! The money! Where was the money? Where the fuck did all these drugs come from?

I started tearing things apart, searching for the cash. I jumped up in disbelief. No way did I lose that money. No way did I go blow it on all these drugs. No way am I that stupid! I fell back on my dirty mattress. I could feel the burning in my nose. Then, a pressure in my lower back. That wasn't normal. I felt some relief as I thought that it could be the money. I flipped the thin mattress to find that half of the $10,000 bundle was gone. I almost screamed in relief but heard footsteps outside so held out. $17,500. That was a great feeling. On that note, I left. Taking the only thing suitable to hide all this stuff, the microwave, and loading it with all the various drugs I had acquired somehow the night before, and of course, the money. Larry was walking down the hill to come to the place. I intercepted him with a simple but stern;

"Larry, walk!"

I pointed the direction and followed him as he scurried up the hill he came. I scurried up behind him, really starting to feel that cocaine.

"Hey Brucie! Where you goin' with the microwave? Larry asks.

I respond quickly, "Shut up Larry, just walk!"

I could smell myself stinking something foul. I really needed a shower. So did Larry. I couldn't go back to the showers. I had to figure something out pretty quickly.

"Hey Larry, were you down by the park today by any chance?" I ask, while slowing him down a little to talk.

"Well yeah, Brucie, I kinda' live down there when I can't crash in the basement. I had to leave because some police were down there, they asked me pretty much the same thing you just did."

My heart sunk.

"Larry, what did they say to you?" I ask.

"Oh just a few questions. Where I was, where I live, if I have an I.D. You know, basic cop shit."

"Did they say what happen?!"

"Yeah." Larry says.

"They said that someone was murdered by the showers, and I guess it was pretty bad, they had detectives and shit. It's pretty scary for a guy like me, I mean jeez, I live down there."

"Larry, did they ask about a suspect?"

"A what?" Larry responds.

"A suspect! Like, a guy that they think it might be!?"

"Oh… sorry Brucie. But yeah, they said they didn't have one. I asked them if they knew if he was still around. The cop said that they didn't know. Something about it being unclear footage for them to see anyone, and there not being cameras in the showers, pretty ironic, huh Brucie?"

"Actually, no, Larry, that's not Irony at all. More like stupidity." I respond.

"Well whatever." Larry responds.

I started going over the details of the night in my head. Could this come back to me? It happened in the shower. It was self defense! Did I leave any evidence? Did I really kill him? Should I do more cocaine?

I had to find out more. So Larry and I went down to a small gas station where I bought a newspaper. Front page: Big font. "Creature from the black lagoon!" It was featuring a slightly distorted surveillance photo of a man covered in sea muck and debris. I walked outside and read the article.

"A Smog Town man, Martin Hogarth, 18, was found dead last night in Ericson Park. A victim of an apparent altercation, he was found dead at the scene as result of asphyxiation. 'Evidence shows no sign of a struggle' detectives on the scene said, 'all we really have to go on is that the man washed ashore and walked to the showers. Almost like out of a movie.' Surely this may come shocking to the family of the deceased Martin Hogarth. Respondents are observing the case to be a possible result of self defense, due to forensic evidence that links skin on the boys hand to that of some found on the brick structure that makes up the showers. This evidence however is a bit confusing and we are working with the park faculty to try and learn more about what happened. Police spokesperson commented, 'If anyone knows anything that pertains to this case or has seen anything, please contact your local authority's as soon as possible.' Hogarth is survived by a younger sister, and his mother."

Holy shit. I couldn't believe it. What about the other people? They were up to no good as well, maybe they will keep quiet. Maybe they were all messed up and won't remember me. All these things plagued my mind endlessly. I had profited big time off that kid. As bad as I felt about what happened, he did come at me first. I just felt horrible because the media and detectives might not see it that way. I wasn't too worried though. They might legitimately be looking for a sea monster for all I know. So there I stood. A microwave full of felonies, Larry, and I. I look at Larry, Larry looks at me. It is time to go. I don't even remember how or where I got all the drugs from. I could be on a list or something.

"Larry, do you know anywhere I can stay for a little bit?" I ask, then immediately remember, Larry typically does not know much.

"Um, let me think Brucie." He pauses for a few seconds. I was just waiting for what was going to come out of his mouth.

"Yeah! Actually I do! This chick I know that comes around the park is always talking about how her grandmother kicked her out for not paying rent or something.. We could find her and see if maybe you could pay the rent and get her old room. I don't know how you will pay the rent, but she said it's available."

It seemed in a way, abrasive and sudden, but I did not really have a choice. I could not do a legitimate lease due to the fact that it was stolen money, and of course because if I dared put money in the bank, my leans and loans would immediately attack it. So pursue this room it was. It could not be that bad.

Larry and I walked near the park. Not exactly where I wanted to be, but I had to try and meet this girl. There was a crowd near the gates for the park. Gawking at what they could see past the tapes and blinders that the police had set up. I slowed up for a moment as Larry perused the crowd for the girl he was looking for. He seems to spot her and signals me to follow. I walk towards Larry and see this poorly shaped young woman sleeping underneath the awning at the nearby bodega. She wasn't bad looking in the face. But you could tell she just did not care about herself.

"Yo! Christy!" Larry yells loudly near her head while nudging her shoulder to try and wake her up;
"Christy! Christiiinaa! Wake up! Wake up bitch!"

She rumbles to life and makes this horrible noise with her mouth, It sounded like "what, Larry?" but it was so gurgled in the phlegm that was stuck in the back of her throat that it sounded like air escaping through mud. Obviously an opiate fan. She clears her throat and tries again.

"What's up Larry?" she asks.

"Hey, what's the deal with that room, is your Grandma still renting it or what?"

"Yeah, it's still open.. Who is your friend?" She asks as she looks at me.

"Cool! Oh, this is my buddy Brucie. He is looking for a room." Larry responds.

"Oh, I see. He's kinda cute!" she says.
All I can think about is how bad she probably smells. Her breath, her ass. All of it.

But, who am I kidding, at this point. I would nail her. I give her this look that was a mix between a thank you and a stern no. Larry smacks her shoulder and gets her attention back.

"Hey! Listen! Where does she live, he needs a place like now!"

I was really proud of Larry at this moment, he took some pretty solid initiative.

"Jeez Larry, relax. She is up on Mumblefree Road. It's a bright blue house, you cannot miss it. Just knock, and tell her that I told ya about the room and whatever."

"Cool, thanks." Larry says.

"Hey Larry, you have any H?" she asks.

Seriously, like Larry had heroin. This girl was a junkie and dumb as hell to top it all off.

"No Christy, and stop asking."

I could not help but laugh. She looks at me.

"How about you buddy, you have any H? I'll drain those balls of yours for twenty…"

Larry interjected.

"NO! We don't have anything Christy! Fuck! Leave the guy alone!"

I kind of wanted to give her the twenty and let her do her thing at this point. Shit, I might of even had some heroin in the microwave. I doubt it though, I never really got into that stuff. Mainly because this Christina chick was a prime example of what it will do to you. I was just desperate and wildly depraved. I did have that weird brown paste though, but I wasn't sure it was anything like that because I hadn't felt any effect from it yet.

"You guys are fuckin' gay!" she says. I couldn't help but laugh. Then, she got pissed because I was laughing.

"Hey asshole, how about this? You give me twenty bucks for telling you about this place or else I go up to my grandmas right now and tell her to tell ya' guys to fuck off!"

I was about to flip out on this girl, but instead of making a scene near the gates I decided to just give her the damn twenty and forget about it.

"Fine! I'll g-"

"Shh.." Larry interjected. He grabbed me and pulled me to the side and began to talk with me in private.

"Your not really gonna' give that to her are you, and where the fuck did you get $20?!" Larry asks.

"Yeah Larry, I was. She wants to be a bitch so I'm just going to give her it, I mean I stole it anyway.." I answer.

"Well dude.. I mean.. If your just gonna' give it to her, what do you say you just hook me up with it, and I'll get a blowy real quick?"

I look at Larry in a strangely humored way and say;
"Sure thing, bud."

I grabbed a wad of money that was in my right front pocket and unwrapped a twenty off of it to present to Larry. Larry's face lit up like a firework as he grabbed the twenty and thanked me for my patronage.

"Holy shit Bruce thank's so much man!"

He about faced like a soldier and walked toward Christy like he had a stick up his ass.

"So Christy!" Larry says.

"I, um.. Got your twenty. Here's the deal. We retracted your second offer, and accept the first. So, I do believe, some nut draining is in order."

"Wait.. For you? Larry?" She asks.

"Yes. For me." He answers.

She looks at me. Then looks at Larry, then back at me. Then back at Larry, and says:

"Well.. Fuck it."

About 15 minutes later Christy and Larry walk out from behind an old abandoned tractor trailer cab. Larry looks as if he was in love. Christy looks like she just gave a blowjob for $20.

"So, can I call you?" Larry asks.

Christy looks puzzled as she hides her smirk.

"Larry, I don't own a fucking phone dude, are you serious?"

Larry stood there crushed as he looked into her eyes and all I could do is laugh a little because to be honest this girl is a train wreck, and Larry was in love with her.

"Well… Fine then." He mumbles as walking away.

Obviously laughing hard at Larry now.

"Hey buddy, she didn't say no." I say comically

"Fuck you, dude!" Larry returned.

I look at Christy.

"Hey, thanks!" I say with my back to her.

She just stood there with a blank look on her face as Larry and I walked away.

Larry and I began our trek across town in search of a bright blue house on Mumblefree Road. Larry seemed unforgiving of this cruel act of nature that he had experienced. He kept saying that "it was amazing and she was a really good girl deep down in her soul." The truly amazing thing is that I could tell he was being genuine. Larry was actually in love with this chick. For some reason, that angers me. Maybe because he was just so damn stupid.

I stopped walking, and Larry did as well but as he turned around to see what was going on I slapped him square across he face and shouted:

"Shut the fuck up about this girl Larry! She is a damn dope fiend and you know it and I know it, for fuck's sake man the whole damn town probably knows it!"

He stood there with his hand on his face and a tear gently forming in the eye of the side I smacked. I stood there a second longer and walked away with Larry in tow. We didn't even make it past the town buildings before he started blabbering on again about this girl.

I turn around abruptly.

"Larry what the fuck man… Do I really have to smack the shit out of you again?!"

He looks at me with a hint of regret to which I sympathized with immediately.

We continue on the trip to find this house and possibly rent out the room that was available, and this was good because I was starting to feel a massive B.M. in the makings and would like to not have to squabble together remnants of whatever available to get the job done. I would like to finally have a legitimate and relaxing bowel movement. I also was getting very tired of lugging around a damn microwave. It was then that I had an epiphany.

"Larry." I stop and say.

"Yeah?" He answers with a puzzled but slightly frightened look in his eyes.

"What the fuck are we doing?" I ask.

"Uhm, I don't know Brucie, you said-"

"No moron, I mean like what the fuck are we *doing*. I am calling a cab and we are getting the fuck out of here." I interjected abruptly.

"Oh Shit! Right on!" He says.

I stood out in the road and flail my free hand while screaming for a taxi. A passing by taxi slams on it's brakes and jams the car in reverse to come snag us. I stood there relieved as the car speeds for me and slams on the brakes again as he stops with the door in front of me. I open the door and get in and Larry follows.

The driver is this 40-something year old man with a scar across his chin named 'Arnelio Montello.' He drives slowly and asks us in his strong accent:

"So where you's goin'?"

"Mumblefree Road." I respond.

"Bumble bee road?! Where the fuck is that?" He asks.

"No, not bumble bee, man. Mumble-free. With an M, an F, and R-"

"Yeah yeah, Mumblefree I heard ya's the first time."

"Oh, alright" I respond. Asshole.

The cab goes silent for a moment before Arnelio says something.

"So, what's you two, couple of fags?"

Larry and I look at each other and then look at this guy before I say;

"What the fuck did you just say to me?"

The driver shows a smile that I can make out through the glass.

"Alright, alright. Just calm down I was just messin' wit' you."

"Oh, alright."

Another moment of silence before Arnelio breaks the silence again.

"Yeah, I think my son is gay, or you know, a fag."

He says the word fag with a touch of mocking remorse for the word. I cannot help but laugh a little at this guy, but he just continues on his rant.

"Lemme' tell ya' something. The other day, my son, he has his birthday right? So a couple a days before, I asks him, Joey, what do ya' want for ya' birthday? You know what that little bastard says to me? He goes, Dad, I wants the new game box or whatever the hell it's called. Can you fuckin' believe that?"

"Nah.. Unbelievable." I respond. Clearly patronizing this man, and he either doesn't care or notice.

"I know right? I mean I just bought him that damn game box last year. Fuckin' thing cost's me two hunnid' dollas'. Now the lil' bastard wants to get a new one?"

"Fucked up." I say.

"Yeah, it is fucked up! I hear him when he's on tha' playin' wit' his friends and they always doing some gay shit playin' whatever."

"Yeah man that's messed up." I say, "How old is your son?"

"He just turned 6 last Tuesday."

Oh man. This kid is doomed. Left with the ever so bright future and positive role model set forth by his low class, homophobic, and suspected alcoholic father.

"Yeah, no shit? That's a good age. I don't remember when I was six but I think it was a good age."

"Yeah, you ain't kiddin' son." Arnelio says.

It is at that point that we had finally cut through all the bullshit and were left alone. Just me, Scary Larry, and a microwave oven full of illegal narcotics. The microwave was getting a little bulky and I really didn't want to be carrying the thing anymore because, well, to be honest, it was stressful. I mean damn, there was probably shit in there that any law enforcement officer would not be able to identify. Shit, I could hardly identify.

We had finally arrived at the home. It wasn't a bad spot. Actually quite nice. It looks a little old but so do the others around it. I could just picture the 50's and 60's era baby-boomers with their smiles, and big boat cars. Loading up the trunk with picnic supplies and fishing poles and mommy's anxiety pills and daddy's six pack of Schlitz and pack of unfiltered cigarettes. Pumping gallons of exhaust fumes into the air as their V8 steel monster blazes its way one and a half miles up the road to the local fishing, camping spot. Ah, America.

I am interrupted from my post hallucinogenic bliss by Arnelio saying:

"Ay' Space cadet, you alive? Listen it's $6.50, you got that man?"

"Oh, yeah, sure Arnelio, here-"

I hand him the cash.

"Hey take it easy man, good luck with the kid." I say.

"Yeah, thank you, y'all have a great day, alright?" He responds.

"Yeah you too."

Larry and I exit the cab and approach the house like it is salvation in front of us.

"Larry!" I say.

"Yeah?" He answers.

"Listen man, I think you better stay out here, you might scare the chick. I mean what is she gonna' think when a dude carrying a microwave and his sloth looking friend come to the door. She is gonna' call the cops!"

"Man, fuck you!" He says.

"No, seriously Larry, just chill here. Please."

"Alright man, alright." Larry says before sliding both his hands into his empty front pockets, of his too tight jeans.

I approach the door. I wonder what this woman looks like. Maybe it will be some cougar of an old woman. Maybe she is an old lesbian type, or some woman with purple hair and a butt plug fetish. Who the hell knows. I mean her granddaughter just blew Scary Larry for almost nothing. I guess I am just hoping for the best. I knock on the door.
Once.
Wait for anything.
I knock again, this time a little harder.

"Hello?!" I yell.

Now I'm getting impatient. I turn around and kick the door three times with the sole of my shoe. Then I heard what sounded like someone clearing their throat and somebody's voice followed after.

"Hold on, hold on I am coming!"

I let out a sigh of relief.

The door opens without anyone at the window glass and I am presented with this little old woman, wheeling herself along with a wheelchair. She is wearing a Sunday dress like she was getting ready to go somewhere and these white gloves that you might see in a 1980's music video.

"Well what do you want?" she asks.

"Oh, um.. Well I had just talked to Christina? She said she's your granddaughter and that you might have a room for rent?"

"Oh, okay, come on in son, here, put your things down by the door and follow me to the kitchen." she says.

As I am stepping through the door the smell of cat urine hits me like a brick to the forehead.
I follow the woman to the kitchen and on the way I notice all of the sentiments and nick-knack's that she has hanging throughout her home. A true testament of sorts to the belief that the things you own end up owning you. She is nice though. We arrive at the kitchen where she had a cup of coffee sitting on the kitchen table where she must have been sitting.

"We have to make this quick, my husband will be picking me up any moment now to go to church. He just ran out to get a new pair of shoes at the five-and-ten cent store."

I hadn't heard someone say "the five-and-ten cent store" since I heard my adoptive mother say it so many years ago. It brought me right back.

"Okay, well, my name is Bruce, and I am from around here. I'm really just looking for a place to stay when I am not working." Yeah, like I have a job.

"Oh, so good, you're working! That is great, because the last couple people have not really worked out. Always a problem with rent, or this or that. One of them, my granddaughter."

"Yeah, I had just seen her and she had told me of the place so we figured we would come check it out."
It is amazing how clean and proper I can transform myself to be when the situation arises to do so.

"Okay sure, follow me," she says before wheeling towards the exit of the room.

"So the rent is seven hundred a month. Electricity and the shower up there are included in the deal. It is an extra fifty a month for refrigerator space and an extra fifty on top of that if you want your laundry done."

Damn, eight hundred a month for clean laundry and fresh food? not too bad. She stops at the bottom of the stairs and says;

"It's up there. First door on the right. Bathroom is at the end of the hall."

"Okay, thank you." I say.

I climb the stairs and realize that there is no assistance for her to get up them because of her wheelchair. What am I walking into. This place could be a wreck. I mean who is taking care of this place? Hopefully the husband that she mentioned earlier takes care of the upstairs area. Regardless, I have no idea what to expect.

I arrive upstairs and follow the directions she gave me. First door on the right. I look into the door, and it is a closet. It's full of what look like old jackets, and the base of the closet loaded with worn shoes and mouse debris. The bathroom was at the end of the hall still so I look behind me and notice another door at the left of the stair landing. I walked to that door and open it, though it gave a little resistance at first. I look inside and am just disgusted. It looks like a couple fiends were living in this room before me. There is needles on the floor and bed. Empty baggies and burned up cotton balls. Blood on the walls and light switches. It is awful in there. But to be honest. It was a hell of a lot better than where I was coming from. Hell, it even has a little TV, not bad.

I close the door and make my way back downstairs to get the woman and explain the situation and tell her I would take the room.

When I arrive at the kitchen, she is not there, so I start to look all over for her. I even check back upstairs. I then remember how small she is in the chair and start to check behind the furniture scattered throughout the house. I am yelling now. Hoping for a response from somewhere. Then I figure, well, maybe her husband came and got her. So I approach the front door to leave. That is when I see her outline, hidden behind a vintage style love seat that was positioned to the right of her front door. It startled me as I say:

"Hey, so I think I will take the room. It's a little bit of a mess, so I'm going to try and clean it."

I stop speaking because I realized she is not responding to my words like she was just a while earlier.

"Ma'am... Ma'am?" I say as I shake her chair.

I loop around her. Still with my hand on the top of her wheelchair and speaking a bit louder now.

"Hey... Hey! Wake up! Ma'am?!"

I feel her wrist and there is no pulse to feel. Her skin is still warm. I jump back in shock. I don't know what to say. The expression on my face turns a bit terrified. What the fuck do I do? Holy shit it looks like she was just getting ready to leave. Then I remember. Her husband will come home and he will take care of this. Should I wait? Damn, what a fucking predicament. I open the door and signal Larry to come over. He runs up to the door and says hello the woman and then gets a little cautious as she doesn't respond.

"She's dead Larry. I was just checking out the room and came down and she was nowhere to be found, and I finally found her right where she is, what do we do, man?!" I say. I am a bit frantic so I spewed out more info then he could likely handle.

"Well does she live alone?" He asks.

"I don't know, dude. She fuckin' just said her husband was out getting shoes or some shit and he would be back and she was waiting for him. I don't know what the fuck to do."

"Well, let's give her like thirty minutes or something and then see if he comes back, right?" Larry says.

Larry is making a lot of sense to me today. I am not sure what it was. Maybe it was that brown paste earlier. Maybe it just brought me right down to his level and that was all it did. 'Larry Paste.' But what happens if Larry eats Larry paste. We would have to find out. Maybe later. We got dead person problems right now.

Thirty minutes had passed as Larry and I raided some of the fridge and pantry. Interesting things in there. Mostly old spaghetti and snack cakes. Nevertheless, we had come to a solid conclusion that thirty minutes is long enough and this guy could be taking a shit somewhere for all we know. So I ask Larry to go find Christina in the meantime. Maybe she could help figure this mess out.

I gave Larry a couple $20 bills and shortly after, he left the house. On a mission to find Christina and probably a beer or something to steal on the way. In the time I have alone I decide to do some looking around, and indulging into some of the activities presented to me by my fine microwave oven. I depressed the "open" button and start looking through the variety of goodies I could get into. I was feeling like smoking a joint so I dug though and eventually found a bag of weed that I can smoke. This was no fuzzy poo-poo shwag. The weed in there is on a whole new level. Unfortunately, there are no rolling papers. So I walk over to the old woman's trash can and scrounged for a soda pop can. A Diet Pep-Pep. Not my first choice but it would work. I gander at the kitchen sink and realized that I could wash the can out before I smoke through it. This makes me feel accomplished for some reason. Though I know it was petty as ever and out of touch, the fact that I had caught a break made me feel successful again. Like I am right back at it. So I wash the can out and proceed to press and shape it into a suitable piece of paraphernalia.

Spectacular. I crush up some of the weed and placed it on the holes I had fashioned, found some matches in the old woman's spice rack, and proceed to get lit.

After one hit, I was almost comatose. I sat there at the window trembling. Damn the weed was strong. The shit was bringing me into all the deepest darkest places of my mind and making me ponder what the hell happened. I could feel my heart race, hear my ears ring, and feel every little cell in my body reacting to this stuff.

Damn!

I have to go to the bathroom of the house and splash some water on my face in an attempt to just calm down or sober up a bit. It was no use. This shit is rocking me.

"No use to fight it." I say

I walk through the kitchen, grabbing a bag of greasy pork grinds the woman had on the counter. A fairly odd choice for me. Who, and what the fuck is a pork grind. They are delicious though.

Suddenly, a knock rang on the door followed by a pissed off female voice telling Larry to "shut the fuck up" as the door swung open. I walk into the living room and see Christina hunching over the dead body of the old woman. She showed almost no emotion as she says:

"Yeah, she's dead."

"Yeah! No shit! We knew that already, we brought you up here to find out what the fuck to do about it." I shout at her.

"Well shit, I don't know man! We have not been so close lately because she didn't like my lifestyle, I am not sure what was going on with her, besides her mental shit."

"Mental shit? Well what about her husband, she said he would be right back and they were going to church, he was out-"

Christina cut me off.

"Yeah, dude. That was it. When I was living here, she would just sit in her chair, with this same dress on saying that my Grandpa was coming to get her. She is fucking nuts dude, my grandpa died like 11 years ago."

My jaw drops.

"Wait, he is dead? Shit." I say as I let out a long exhale and grab the back of my neck as I could feel the stress start to form.

Larry had this look of confusion on his face and had the balls to ask:

"Well, how did he die?"

Christina turns around and gives him a very dirty look.

"Fuck you Larry!" She yells.

"Look I just wanted to fucki-"

Christina cut him off:

"No, fuck you Larry, you're a piece of shit you make me sick you fucking asshole!" She yells at him

Oh, young loves. I couldn't help but laugh a little at them.

"You weren't sayin' that when you were suckin' my dick!" I heard Larry say before I had to cut them off.

"Will both of you shut the fuck up! There is a body here alright?! We need to figure this out first. Then you two can bicker!"

They shut up.

"Yeah, you're right." She says.

She kneels back down and grabs her Grandmother's hand. A look of slight remorse in her eye, that and what appeared to be the subtle effects of the heroin in her system.

"I'm sorry Nana' I am just so sorry." She says.

I couldn't help but roll my eyes a little. The situation was just so far gone at this point. Half of me wanted to just slap the hell out of her, half of me wanted to let her cry. So instead, I just sucked it up and made my voice clear.

"Listen Christina, I know that this is a tough thing for you to swallow, but she has been dead now for almost 3 hours and we have to do something before… well, you know" I say with a slight shrug of encouragement.

She looks at the floor, closes her eyes, and lets out a deep exhale. She postures up and begins speaking as she raises herself off the floor:

"…Jeez. Man why today. Ugh. Well, alright. Here is what we gotta' do."

She wipes a long bead of snot from her nose and I can see the long reflective line go up her hand. This girl was so gross.

"Okay guys look, we have to get rid of the body. I think I know this guy-"

"What!?" I interject.

"Don't even fuckin' say it Christina. We can't just get rid of her fucking body, dude. What the fuck is wrong with you?" I say.

"Hey man, listen to me! You're not listening!" she says.

I throw my hand over my mouth and jaw and shook my head at her as if whatever she was going to say was going to justify the fact that she wants to dispose of her grandmothers body, be it also in some weird exotic back alleyway.

"Look, she is my Nana' okay? What I was going to say was we have to get rid of her. If my family finds out she is dead, than they start the process and I will get fucked out of all her shit. She hated me in the last couple years and I am pretty sure she cut me out of her will and everything."

My brain might as well have been on the floor. I was so close to beating this little drug addict's face in. I wasn't exactly a model human being, but what this girl was saying was so damn foul that I couldn't help but say something to her.

"So let me get this straight. You want to take the body of your recently deceased, widowed Grandmother. Get her in the hands of some fucked up back room body disposal, and rob her house so that your cousins and shit don't get anything from her will?"

"Yeah, pretty much." She responds.

"You're a piece of shit!" I say. Instantly realizing that those words did not do justice. "You're seriously the most fucking horrible person I have ever met. Dispose of her body? Yeah no fucking way bitch! I am calling the wagon."

"No! Wait! Okay, maybe what I said was a little fucked up." She admits reluctantly.

"A little?! Look, you need help. Seriously."

Larry was looking at her with such a face of disgust that I thought he might have had a stroke.

"Christina. I am not helping you do that. Even if you weren't some druggie whore that just sucked off my friend for money. Even if you were queen bee. I still wouldn't help your ass!"

She had this look on her face, like a full grown woman mixed with a 7 year old girl who was just stung by a bee on the playground. It was actually quite amusing to see her freaking out in her own way. Drug addicts deserve to be criticized. Deep down, I think they really want to be anyway.

"Look, I am calling the fuckin' ambulance. They are going to come and get her and I suggest you stay put Christina. At least until your family shows up."

"Yo! Fuck that!" she says.

She pushes Larry out of the way and makes a run for the door. Leaving her stink in her wake.

"Man, what the fuck was that, Larry?"

He looks at me with a look of confusion and shaking his head he says.

"Dude I have no fuckin' clue."

I head to her kitchen to use the phone I had seen earlier. I hated dialing those numbers for the emergency services. It was just not unfamiliar to me. I remembered back to a time when I was young in the house and a couple kids thought it would be funny to attack the new kid. This kid, who was transferred into that home for only a couple days while he was in escrow of being adopted by some family upstate. These kids were older, about 16 if I remember right, and they thought it would be funny if the 3 of them got a hold of this 12 year old kid and held him on the ground while the biggest of them, this heavy kid Marco Elioskavich, would draw on his face. It wasn't the first time Marco did this. That walking piece of trash Marco would do this routinely to the newest kids in the home. His two buddies, Josh and Alex, were orphan twin brothers who parents both blew up in a methamphetamine lab related explosion when the boys were 5 years old. Marco was just a total thug. My second day in that place, the 3 of them took turns smacking me in the back of the head for a day. Such assholes. Karma is a bitch though. So this new kid was being held down when Marco starting drawing his favorite images on the boy's face in ball point pen. A swastika, a few dicks, you know, the non creative trash you would see in a truck stop somewhere. I was fortunate enough to be in the corner of the room on my bed reading when this was happening. I was really tired of Marco's shit. I never got it too bad from him because we were around the same age and I think he knew that I wouldn't take much of his shit before flattening his nose. So I said to Marco:

"Yo Marco, get off the fuckin' kid."

They paused for only a second to look at me before the kid they were holding broke free of the two brothers grip and punched Marco directly in his right temple. At the same time, the boy's flailing legs broke Josh's nose and took out his front teeth. Alex was lucky enough to get back quick enough to get away clean. Marco, like the little bitch he was, took the hit to the temple like it was the worst thing in the world. The 12 year old rolled him over and picked the ball point pen that was beside Marco's head and in only a split second starting stabbing the living hell out of Marco's face. Alex was standing against the wall with serious terror in his eyes. I had this feeling of extreme joy to see this kid just destroy these bullies like that.

Josh was rolling around in a pool of his own blood that was pouring from his face like a river. I don't think I have ever seen so much blood. It was crazy. Marco ended up the worst. He was blinded in 1 eye, had all types of nerve damage, lost a few of his front teeth and had horrible scars all over his face. Not to mention a pretty serious concussion that left his with a weird twitch in his neck. The three of them were also charged as adults and spent the next 5 years in the county jail for assault on a minor. I remember the kid getting up, with blood all over his clothes, face, and the pen. He just looks at me and said one thing.

"Thanks."

I had to go call the emergency services soon after. It was also me who had to give a deposition on behalf of the incident. Though it was a pretty clear cut case. The kid had bruises all over him, and to top it all off the proof was drawn all over his face. Marco seriously had it coming. So, Karma's no joke.

I had the numbers dialed, and the respondent on the other end when I gave them the address and felt the immediate panic. What if the respondent identified me as the swamp monster thing? Shit, have to hide the drugs.

"Larry! Quick! Grab the microwave!" I yell to him.

The woman on the other end heard me say that and said:

"I'm sorry sir?"

"Err, um. Nothing... Well I guess I should explain. I was just about to move in to this house when I was taking a tour and found the home owner dead."

"Okay sir, how long has she been unresponsive?"

"I'm not sure, maybe, three hours or so?"

"Okay sir, what is the address?"

"Shit, I'm not sure of the number, I know it's Mumblefree Road. Just hold on I will go find a number."

"Okay sir."

I see Larry walking into the kitchen with the microwave and he places it on the table. I see some mail on a chair in the kitchen and pick it up. A piece of junk mail about a free knee brace. Typical. 67. Alright.

"It's 67, 67 Mumblefree Road."

"Okay sir, we will have someone there within the hour. Please stay at the residence and explain the situation to the first responders."

"Cool, thanks. I will."

"Goodbye sir."

"Bah-Bye."

"Fuckin' within the hour? What the hell is that?" I say.

"Bruce I got the Microwave" Larry says.

"Alright cool, we gotta' hide it man, the first responders are going to be here soon."

We walk to the back of the house to look for a backdoor to a backyard. Found what lead to a backyard that was overgrown and had a shed in the back of it. I could start to hear the ambulance sirens and whistles of other officers in the area.

"Larry, quick man, go hide the microwave in that shed underneath some shit or something. So you can't see it, okay? You know what I mean?"

"Yeah, I gotcha' Brucie."

I head back inside and move to the front of the house to wait for the first responders to arrive. When I got back I peaked through a front window to see an ambulance arriving. 2 men jumped out of the back of it while the driver parked it on the side of the road. I could hear Larry come back into the house just before the men knock on the door. I let them in quickly and they found the body immediately in front of the door, felt for a pulse and confirmed that she had been dead for a little while now. Rigor mortis had set in and her skin is now very pale. One of them grabs the radio off his lapel and says:

"Ten thirty-three, ten thirty-three. Responders call for a ten seventy-nine at 67 Mumblefree, that's 67 Mumblefree."

He looks at me and says,

"How long has she been out?"

"I think about 3 hours now." I answer.

I can see more responders and police arriving now. Great, maybe we should have just donated her to the back alley. I have a strong dislike for cops. Especially when my livelihood is on the line. They all were entering the home now and responding on their radios. It was something else. I want to just be a fly on the wall here and it was working well. Until I see a familiar face enter the house. It looks like a guy I used to know from work way back when I was selling pagers. He looks over in the corner and I lock eyes with him. It couldn't be...

"Louie?" I say quietly.

I see him smile and walk over to me. I shake his hand as he says:

"Holy shit Brucie, It's been a while."

Louie was a fucking cop now. Yeah, that's just perfect. Louie was selling pills about twenty years ago. A real dirty dealer too. Most dealers wait for customers, Louie would spend his time outside grade schools, playgrounds, skate parks, public pools. He was a real piece of shit. The only reason I knew him was because he would buy a new pager every few weeks. Trying to cover his tracks I suppose. It was only right that he was now a cop.

"What's going on Louie, I didn't know you were a cop now. When did this happen?" I ask.

"Oh shit man, I know right? It's been about a year now. It's been good though." He responds.

"Cool, cool." I say.

"Yeah. They got me on the K-9 unit! It's pretty fuckin' cool man!" He says while laughing.

"No shit?!" I say. I could see the people behind him begin to place the woman on a gurney for the ride to the coroner. Larry was walking over to me from the other end of the room.

"Larry, this is Louie, he's a cop… I guess."

"What's up Louie." He says while shaking his hand. I could see a little bit of a brown colored film on Larry's teeth. Larry had gotten into the Larry Paste. Oh shit. This should be fun.

"Hi Larry, Nice to meet you man. So, Bruce, why don't you follow me outside." Louie says.

"Uh, what?" I ask.

"Yeah, we just need to get a formal statement on exactly what happened so we can contact the family and whatever."

"Oh, alright yeah no problem." I followed him outside to the K-9 equipped cruiser that he was driving. The windows were up inside the car and it was hot as hell outside. The dog looked like it is going to pass the fuck out. I ask to pet the dog so maybe he would take it out of the car. Larry was looking at the dog like it was his fucking long lost brother so I knew he would like to play with it as well.

"Louie lets see this fucking dog dude, what is it a drug sniffer?"

"Alright man." he says laughing.

"Yeah, he's a drug sniffer. Drugs, explosives, you know."

"Cool! That's really cool man." I say.

He unlocks the rear door and lets the dog jump down while attaching a leash to its collar.

"Hey pup' pup." I say while petting the dog's back.

It was smelling my pants quite vigorously. There was probably shit on those pants that dog had no idea of what they were. I could see that Larry paste having it's effect on Larry. His eye's are getting all wide and rolling all over his sockets. He looks as if someone would look if they had drank a bottle of tequila on their own.

"Hey Larry, Come check out the dog!" I say.

Larry walks over stumbling and I can see Louie give him this look like he was ready to pounce on him. Larry stomps over to the dog with one open hand and says:

"Hey, doggi-"

Before literally emptying his entire stomach onto this poor dogs head and body.

Louie handed me the dogs lead and pushed Larry to the ground. Larry fell like a tree and just hit the ground sleeping. That Larry Paste was no joke. The poor dog was whimpering and trying to clean all the damn vomit off of itself.

"Holy shit dude!" I say, laughing.

"What the fuck just happened!?" Louie asks.

I felt somewhat bad for the dog but at least it was eating. It made me wonder. Would it get high off of Larry's puke and be a dirty drug dog. Stealing the drugs it sniffs off of people. Finding and cutting the evidence.

"Damn! What the hell am I supposed to do about this!" Louie says. He looks around himself. "Ah ha!"

He reaches down to Larry and pulls the T-shirt off him so he can use it to clean the vomit off of the dog. As he is cleaning the dog he begins talking to me about the incident. Asking why I was there. How I knew her. Basic cop shit. He told me that they already knew who the woman was and that she had a long hospital care record and she was on home care. The family has already been notified, and unless there was evidence of foul play, that I was free to go. This was good news. Nobody cared about Larry, nobody cared about the mass amount of drugs hidden on the property. Nobody even batted an eyelash at the fact that I would be living there. We are golden.

Before long all the authorities had left. I got Larry on his feet and got him over to the curb of the house. I sat him down on the steps and went inside to grab the guy a glass of water, after all he certainly needed something. He crashed harder than anyone I had ever seen before. When I came back out I noticed a car pulling up. A little white sports car. The windows are tinted so I can't see inside. The car parks and the door opens and a foot falls from the door. A little white toe-less high heel shoe with 2 white straps. Pink toe nail polish complimenting her lightly tanned skin. A head pops from the door revealing a woman with long dirty blonde hair. Big luscious lips with a deep red lipstick. She had on these white big framed sunglasses that hid her high cheek bone and smoky eye color. She stood up from the car and looks over to me. I was numb looking at her. She walks towards me. Those long legs barely fitting in the low riding pencil skirt she had on. Arms swinging to those incredible breasts being pressed together by the mid cut camisole. Who the fuck was she.

"Hey! You!" She says.

I look around to make sure this girl is talking to me. Apparently she is. So like a high school boy with a boner in his gym shorts, I respond:

"Uh, yeah?"

"Who the fuck are you and who the hell is this greasy fuck with no shirt on disgracing my mothers house?!"

She was sassy. I like it in a way. So I smiled a bit when I say:

"Whoa, whoa, whoa! Wait a second. Let's us all just calm down. We have all been through a lot here today, I am sure. Hey, and to be honest I think it's fair to say my friend here hasn't exactly had a good one either."

"Fair enough." She says with a bit of sass like she is starting to like me.

She looks around and locks eyes on a police officer and looks him up and down like she wanted to jump into that car with him.

This is Christina's mother? My goodness. I could almost see a resemblance to her. She was stunning. In a totally unnatural and purely cosmetic way. That was when I realized that her daughter just blew Larry for a twenty spot. That's when this woman lost some of her appeal.

"So anyway, this is my mother's house. I just want to know what the hell is going on. You know what I mean?"

"Yeah, yeah! I totally understand. Well anyway, I'm Brucie. I was renting the room. I seriously just moved in here like today. Christina told me about the place."

She didn't at all seem phased about what I said.

"Okay.. Well you don't seem too dangerous so I will take your word for it. But seriously, can you please clean up this guy sitting on the curb here. I mean what the fuck?!"

She squatted down quickly and took her sunglasses off to start screaming at Larry.

"HELLO! GET THE FUCK UP!" She then turns to me and asks, "What did you say his name was?"

"Larry!" I respond, laughing while doing so.

"LARRY! GET THE FUCK OFF THE CURB LAARRRYY!" She yells.

"Call him Scary Larry. He loves that."

"He *likes* to be called Scary Larry?"

"Fuck you Bruce" mutters from Larry's lips.

"Nice... Hey listen Larry you gotta' get the fuck up buddy."

"Are we there yet?" He asks me.

The lady laughed and stood back up. I dropped Larry a hand to help him get up.

"Yeah Lar' we're there."

I walked his wobbly Larry body to the step of the house and he plopped down on it. I definitely heard his tailbone hit the ground. It didn't matter at that point. He was so messed up you could probably take out his liver and he wouldn't even notice. Outrageous.

"So you know Christina?" The woman asks.

"Yeah, I know her, she is... a nice girl?"

"Psh, yeah a nice girl, huh?" she answers with a slight grimace. "You think she is nice? She is a fuckin' drug addict. Drove her poor grandmother up the fuckin' wall. She had her own problems, you know? She didn't need Christina's ass up in here causing all types of shit."

I can feel the heartfelt family story coming. A familiar feeling of discomfort and lack of interest. A lot of agreeing nods and responsive laughter is in order.

"Oh yeah I bet." I ssay, with a nod and a caring look.

"That fuckin' girl was once shooting up on the toilet in her house, mind you she only has one toilet and a very weak bladder. Her druggy ass passes out on the toilet for 4 hours as my poor mother is rapping on the door with her hand. Screwed her hand up. Not to mention my mother pissed all over herself and had to wait until Christina got up before she could clean herself up."

"Oh my fuck?! That is messed up, man." I say.

"Yeah! It's totally messed up."

A break of silence. I cleared my throat and Larry came to life mumbling something about French Toast.
"Oh, looks like your friend is alive!" She says.

"Yeah, looks like it." I say while taking a knee and making sure he isn't about to start sleep walking.

"LARRY! YOU GOOD?!"

"Yeah Brucie! Fuck! What are you yelling for?"

"Ah, good." I say.

I get up and glance at the woman standing above me.

"So, you must be Brucie." she says.

"Yeah that's me!" I present my hand to shake her hand.

"Okay, well, I'm Carmen." she says.

"Nice to meet you Carmen." I say, as she pauses for a bit.

"Nice to meet you too. Listen, I need to go find my daughter, but it has been nice. I will likely be around more because we will have to clean out the house and all. So I will see you around. I'm trusting that you will be take care of this place in the time being."

Was she kidding? Yeah, trust me. I'll take care of the house.

"Yeah, of course. I will" I respond.

"Okay, perfect. I'll see you around, Brucie."

My heart fluttered a little bit as she walked away. My goodness, her body was unbelievable. She was like a sculpture. I look down to Larry and grab his hand to help him stand up. He rose up to his feet and rolls his ankle almost immediately.

"Argh!" he hollered as his bulbous body slammed back to the hard ground.

"Larry! Shit, man! Are you alright?" I say with a hint of laughter.

"No I'm not fuckin' alright! I just broke my ankle! Ahh!" He says, in obvious pain.

"You didn't fuckin' break it Larry. You just rolled it. You will be fine."

"No! It's broken Bruce! It's fuckin' broken!"

"Alright, alright Larry! Relax! Just wait here a second I will be right back, and try to be quiet man people are looking at us!" I say.

"Alright just hurry up!" He responds.

I ran inside the house, ran out the back door, and located the very poorly hidden microwave oven that Larry had clearly just placed in the middle of everything inside the shed. It didn't matter. I opened the microwave and located the wonderful off-brown "Larry Paste" and brought it back out front to Larry.

"Here Larry, this will help."

I dipped my finger in the paste and shoved it into Larry's mouth. He didn't care in the least. He swallowed the glob and I helped him back to his feet and stumble into the front room of the house so he could sit down.

"Alright buddy, Just wait here, I will call the ambulance. Just give me a minute to find the phone."

I go right back out the back door and put the Larry Paste back and grab the bag of weed that was in the microwave. Some very fine weed. Wonderful. There was even a pack of papers I didn't notice before stuck in the back of the microwave. So I rolled up a small joint. It had been a long day and I was ready to relax, damn it. I found an old bucket near the shed and flip it over. I sat there for a minute and broke up some of the weed. Got a paper out of the packet and roll up and nice sized joint.

No fire.

"Fuck!" I proclaimed.

Check the microwave. Nothing. I'm looking around the shed, and notice a blow torch with an old spark igniter hanging on the wall next to it. Both, obviously very old with little chance of the igniter working. I grab the tank. Half full. Grab the igniter, and held it in my hand.

"Please work,"
I hold the clamp, retract the handle, and bingo!
"Yes!"

I turned the twist valve on the torch and the damn handle snaps off.

"You have got to be fucking kidding me!" I proclaim as I shoot off the bucket stool and head back to shed to try and find a pair of pliers to open the valve. Only finding a pair of rusty old pliers with one handle snapped off. I found this quite ironic. Maybe they were born for each other. No matter. They will work. I head back out to the bucket and open the valve to the tank. Spark the igniter and light the torch.

"Nice!"

I feel around my ear, check my lap. No joint.

"What the FUCK!" I yell.

I kill the torch, and jump off my seat and start tearing into the shed to try and find my joint. Found a few old nick-knacks but no damn joint. Must have been at it ten minutes before I quit.

"Ah fuck it!" I say, walking out of the shed.

There is the joint. Sitting right next to where I was sitting.

"HA! Wow."

I sparked the joint and sat there pondering what the hell it was that brought upon this strange coincidence it was that I ended up at this exact moment. It was scary to be honest. How frightened I used to be in my youth. Of the future, the unknown. How everything was going to play out for me and what would be the answer in the end. I take another puff. Thinking slightly about the way it all went down. What decision did I make to be the guy that I was. I wanted to stop thinking like this, as it started to upset my stomach and I felt a touch of anxiety begin to present itself.

"Nope."

This was not going to happen. Let the smoke subdue you. You're fine. Just chill.
I stared at the sun. It was warm. The world was spinning the way it should have and everything was right and true. What else was there to worry about. Nothing. I was so small and irrelevant on a universal scale that it made me feel correct. Fuck, I mean what if everything was just a bad simulation. Never mind. I'll go inside.

"Oh shit, Larry!"

I stand up and go into the house and see Larry just chilling out on the couch watching television.
I decided to sit down next to Larry and kick it for a while with him. His ankle was definitely messed up. We will give it some time. I laid back and eventually fell asleep.

I had a dream. It was very interesting and vivid. A beach. Open and dark. A full moon that seemed unbelievable and huge. Waves crashing and half of the beach was being pounded by an extremely viscous storm. I look at the ground quickly. It was glowing as if the sun was reflecting off of it. Yet everything was still dark. I heard my voice and began to look behind me when I heard a phone ringing and I woke up.

"Fuck!"

I rub my eyes and walk in the direction of this ringing menace.

"Fuck You!"

I pick up the phone and mumble a nasty "*Hello*" into the receiver.
It was someone screaming at me in what sounded like Mandarin Chinese.

"Whoa whoa! Y'all need to chill!"

They didn't acknowledge my words, so I just hang up.

The phone kept ringing.

I pick it up.

"Hello!?"

Asian screaming.

"What the *fuck*?"

I hang up.

The phone keeps ringing, so I just walk away.

"Larry I'm leaving."

Larry mumbles a bit.

I walk down to Smog Town. Headed to a bar for a few drinks and hopefully a few laughs. I should get a damn car. Walking sucks. Especially when your shoes suck and have holes worn to the skin on your foot. Listen to me trying to act like I wasn't a damn hobo again. As I step into the bar I am greeted by a few people who know me from around town.

"Yo, Brucie! Whats happening man?" says one of the gents at the bar.

I greet him with a hand.

"How you doing, Bobby?" I ask.

"Good, good. Yourself?" He responds.

"I'm solid, just living." I say as I sit down on the bar stool. The bartender asks.

"So, what will it be Bruce?"

"I'll have a Schlitz."

She reaches under the bar and grabs a beer to open it with her key ring.

"Thanks"

I sip my beer and watch the football game that was being played on the screen at the bar. Overhearing the conversations going on right next to me. Stories about nights that have passed and the fun they have been. Certain scenarios. Some I remember, some I don't. I overhear them reminiscing about a time when this guy Gary, who got a little bit too drunk one night and then took a piss in the corner of a bar up the street. *Then,* proceeded to go into the bathroom and black out on the floor wrapped around the dirty toilet bowl while singing a song by The Kinks.

It was at that moment when a man named Al walks in saying something about how someone robbed his backpack out of his car. He was pretty pissed about it. I suppose he had some weed and money, or something in it worth getting back.

"We gotta' get my fucking shit back!" He says. He was livid, red in the face, and shaking mad.

I really sympathized with this dude. I feel for him. I have had a few things stolen from me in my life so it hit me. I guess the beer made me a little courageous.

I jumped to it and say:

"Yeah man, let's go find your shit!"

Some guy raised his voice at the end of the bar.

"Hey, I don't know if it means anything, but I saw two kids walking through the parking lot like 10 minutes ago when I was smoking a cigarette."

"No shit? What did they look like?" I ask.

"I don't fuckin' know man. They looked like some young douche bags. Fuckin' khakis on one of him. Sagging his pants hard." He answers.

"Black, White, Latino, what were they?"

"A couple white kids, they went into McGregors."

'McGregors' was this hole in the wall Irish pub with a solid selection of soccer mom tail if you go in on a week day.

"Alight cool. Let's go."

Al and I went into McGregors and asked the bartender Mike if he had seen the two kids. Mike knew immediately who we are talking about and went on to tip us off to them.

"Yeah, those two were here. They sat at the bar for a little while on their cell phones looking at train schedules. Then, one of the little assholes tried to buy a drink with a fake I.D. and I had to kick them out."

He looks at us and asks:

"Why?"

"Dude, those kids robbed my car, I think. Did they have a backpack with a metal water bottle and Frisbee sitting out the back pockets?" Al asks.

"Yeah, dude, actually they did! It is funny that you ask because they kept rummaging through the bag while they were sitting there, and the water bottle fell out and slammed into the bar." He answers.

I told Al to get on his phone and look up the next train leaving Smog Town. He looks at his phone and does some quick research and finds that there is a train leaving Smog Town Station in 30 minutes.

"It's leaving in 30 Brucie" Al says "should we go down there?"

"Well if you want your shit back, yeah Al, I think we should."

He let out a reluctant breath and says:

"Well alright, than let's go."

We head for the door to make our exit and head to the train station in an attempt to find these punks. Honestly, who steals anymore? Well, besides me. Especially in little old Smog Town. The place in no bigger than a Hamlet and when you fart everybody in town smells it, or at least it feels that way. It wouldn't be long now before we had these perpetrators in our midst.

As we exit the building, we are confronted by another local acquaintance. A familiar faced guy that everyone knew as Drew. I think it was short for Andrew. Everyone always joked about this guy and his character because he once was wasted off of dark rum on Christmas Eve and thought it would be a good idea to run around his mothers house tearing all of her things off the wall and really just destroying the inside of her home. She actually had to call the cops and have him forcefully removed. He was so drunk though, that when the cop grabbed him, he swung a punch at the officer and the cop responded with a dropping blow to the neck. Drew called the cop a pussy as he was forced into the backseat of the cop car. While in the cop car he laid on his back and started kicking the window out of the back door. After about 2 minutes of kicking with no success breaking the glass, his pants had fallen to his knees. Being as drunk as he was it doesn't really pain me to say that the guy proceeded to piss his entire bladder all over the cop car's rear seats and floor.

After that, he had my respect.

Drew spoke.

"Yo, I heard someone robbed your shit out of your car!"

It struck me as a bit strange that Drew knew this already. I assume he was just next door and heard something about what had happened.

"Yeah dude, it's fucked up, we are about to go find the people who did it and get my shit back." Al answers.

"Word. Can I roll with you guys?" Drew asks.

"Yeah man, let's go" Al says.

We walk over to Drew's car and drive quickly over to the train station to try and find these guys.
When we arrive Al and Drew quickly exit the car, with a slightly buzzed and tired me following casually behind. The two bolt quickly up the ramps to the train that was sitting and waiting as it was scheduled to leave shortly. I watched eagerly over the exits of the train. Observing to find any passengers exiting the train as they witness any commotion. I walk quickly towards the rear end of the train looking inside the windows to see what was going down. The air became still and quiet as I focused dramatically on Al and Drew as they walked up and down the isles of this double decked train. They make contact. I start to feel that primal rage feeling in my stomach. That feeling like you just caught the animal prey that has been tormenting your famished stomach for days. It was on.

Al and Drew pulled these two out of the train by their shirts and proceed to push them off the train. I run up on the group and say:

"Are these the two that stole your fuckin' backpack bro?"

"Yeah!" Al answers

.

"Look!" He says as he points to the back pack in the kid's hand.

"Oh! No shit?! Well let's go for a little walk!" I say as I push one of the punks in the direction I wanted them to move.

The men began to march. We escorted these two off of the train ramps and towards the park entrance that was just east of the train station. The two getting bombarded by slurs and questioning the entire time. I would have been shaking if I were one of these kids. They are obviously scared. But it is almost in disbelief. They couldn't believe that they didn't get away with this petty crime.

We escort the thieves to the pavilions in the park. When we get there we shake them down for what they have.

One of the thieves says something.

"Look, I don't know what is going on but-"

Al interrupts,

"Shut the fuck up! You know why you are here. You know what the fuck you did. Just give me back my shit and we won't fuck you up!"

Al is red with anger.

"Oh..oh, okay!" The thief says.

"Give me my fucking back pack!" Al says as he yanks it out of the hand of the one thief.

Drew then demands that the two give them their wallets. Which they do. He reaches into the bill fold and takes out the two boy's identification cards.

"Okay who do we got here," Drew says.

He looks down at the I.D. cards and squints to read the names.

"We got a, Charles Salazar, and a, hmm, Michael McCormic."

"Charlie, and Mike." Al says.

"You're from East Parkland huh?" He asks.

That was when Drew snapped.

"You little fucks come into my fuckin' town and break into a car and steal my friends shit?!" He yells.

Drew grabs one of the thieves by the collar of his shirt and punches him in the stomach.

"Drew, chill!" Al says.

He looks at Al and I and pushes the guy into the cement divider located directly behind him. The thief's back slams hard into the cement beveled edge and he lets out a loud cry as he falls to the ground.

"My fucking back!" The thief cries.

"Get the fuck up! You're fine!" Drew demands.

It was then that we noticed that there are two older men running towards us. I immediately acted on this and began to approach the men quickly. I wasn't really sure what I was thinking when I essentially just threw my hands in the air and started screaming at the top of my lungs. The two men see me do this and immediately back track quickly before saying,
"Fuck that!"

They walked away quickly. I felt tough, but they really just saw a scruffy homeless looking man come at them all crazy. They likely just feared I would stab them with a syringe or something. I turned around to see Al screaming in the face of one of the thieves. Drew was doing the same but had his hand around the collar of the kid and was shaking him awfully hard. The kid was obviously in a lot of pain. I look at this happening and immediately felt a sense of sorrow. That always happens to me after LSD experiences. A general dislike and uncomfortable sense of detachment for these types of aggravated emotion. I could feel the emotion run from my face as I gazed down upon this happening. I couldn't believe any of this, it was just too surreal. What is this? Who are we? Why the fuck should I even care about this? It's a backpack. Not the end of the world. Though I suppose I wish it was the end of the world. The end of all the bullshit. All the pain.
Another time.

"Ah fuck it." I say, as I snap back to reality.
The man in me was ready to combat this aggressive behavior. I think the two had learned the lesson long ago, and Al and Drew are now just releasing pent up aggression on the two thieves.

"Yo! Chill out Al! Chill the fuck out! Both of you!"
They look up at me like a pair of hyenas that had an unwanted guest approach their meal.

"I mean seriously, cool the fuck out. Have you guys even looked in the bags to make sure your shit is still in there?" I ask.

They look puzzled.

"No man, but they have the bag-" He says, as I interrupt.

"Dude, just make sure your stuff is even in it."

I am relieved to see I had cut the thieves a quick break. The one who took a blow to the back was rolling around in severe pain. I gaze upon him. There did not appear to be any blood, at least not on the outside.

Al opens up the backpack to find that some of his possessions are missing. This is where I immediately regret even mentioning the comment to check the contents of the bag.

"Dude, what the hell? Where is my shit?!" He yells.

"What do you mean?" I ask.

He looks down into the bag and shuffles some of the contents around.

"I had some of my clothes and shit in here, it was like a day bag. Yeah, and my weed is missing! I had a pill bottle with a quarter ounce in it."

Al walks over to the thief who was checking on his friend at the moment. Al snapped a little bit as he cocked back his right foot and kicked the thief in the side of the face. To which he was returned with the thief letting out a short winded gasp.

"Where's my fucking stuff?!" He yells.

"We dumped it! We dumped it." The thief answers with slight disorientation.

"Where the fuck did you dump it?" Al asks.

"We dumped it over by the docks... The docks."

Al calls the thief an asshole and runs over to the docks. About 100 yards away. I look over at Drew who was sitting on the park bench in the pavilion looking down at the two thieves. The one with the back injury was in a substantial amount of pain.

"Hey, you. What is your name?" I ask him.

"Charlie" He answers, with pain in his voice.

"Ah," I add "So that means that *you* must be Mike." As I point at the swollen cheek of the thief sitting above him.

"Yes, I'm Mike." He says.

I notice his face was beginning to swell up.

"You know you guys kinda' fucked up, right?" I say.

"Yeah, I know." Mike answers, as he coughs in an agonized manner.

Charlie was beginning to moan and cry with pain.

"Is he going to be alright? Your friend seems to be in a lot of pain and I think he might have to be for a while as you two are getting on the next train out of here and going home. Is that understood?"

"Yes." Mike says.

"I said, is that understood!" I yell in the direction of Charlie.

"Yes!" Charlie proclaims.

"Good! Now we are heading out of here. A word of advice to the both of you. Don't steal." I say.

Yeah, me telling these boys not to steal. Hypocrite. Shit, just the other day I was stealing chocolate bars to munch on in the basement of a place I wasn't renting and using a stolen toaster oven, powered via a stolen extension cord transporting stolen electricity to heat up my more than likely stolen food.

Al was running back towards the pavilion with a bunch of random objects bundled in the front of his shirt like a makeshift hammock.

"You get it all?" I ask.

"Yeah. I mean minus the granola bar I had in the pocket, which I am sure one of these little fuckers ate already." Al says with a face of genuine disgust. He was rather broken up about that. I understand though. Food is life.

I gave him a relieved look and shrugged my shoulders.
"Not too bad." I say

He agreed, and the three of us banded together and walked out of there as quickly as possible. Hoping that the two boys had the nerve to get on the next train, and of course, keep quiet to authorities.
As we are walking back to Drew's car we noticed that the sun was coming up. It instilled a hint of comfort, in a mildly exhausting way. The type of feeling that you get when you win. The type of feeling you experience when things go your way, even for a second. It was incomparable. The world was still for just a second between us.

We all got into Drew's car.

"So what are we doing for food." I ask.

"I was just about to ask you the same thing." Al answers.

"Yo, y'all want to get some waffles?" Drew asks.

Al and I both respond quickly with "Fuck yeah."

We are off. But not before stopping at the local gas station and getting the three for $5, 22 ounce Schlitz light special.

We arrive at the waffle house and had a nice buzz going when we got there. We all drank down the 22 ounce's like it was water in the desert, so on an empty stomach, it certainly had good effect.

"I want some fuckin' french fries." Al says.

We walk in and have a seat.

"So what are y'all thinking." I say.

Upon sitting down we are approached by a very bashful waitress. Her name tag says her name was Hannah but she definitely looks like a Tiffany. She spoke with a spot of remorse as she asks us what we wanted. The three of us look at her simultaneously and then quickly look down. Al looks up and clears his throat.

"I'm gonna' get an English breakfast with extra bacon and a side of hash browns and gravy." Drew says.

"That sounds dope. I'm gonna' get the same." I add.

Al coughs and lifts his head up.

"Mannn, I just want some french fries and a whole pickle…" Al says. "… and please, no salt on the fries!" He adds.

Drew and I look at him very puzzled.

"Why the hell are you ordering fries without salt? They taste like shit without salt." Drew asks.

"Yeah and what the fuck? Like, a whole pickle?" I ask him

The waitress looks at us with a slight smirk.

"Yeah, like a whole pickle?" She asks.

"Yeah, like a whole damn pickle, please." He answers.

"Well, alright, how about anything to drink?"

"I'll have a ginger ale." Drew says.

"Yeah that sounds good, I'll have a ginger ale as well." I say.

Drew gave me a sideways dirty look and shrugged his shoulder. Basically like I stole his whole order. I just look at him and laugh.

"Um, you got beer?" Al says.

Drew and I look at each other wide eyed then look over at him.

"Seriously Al, it's like 9 a.m." Drew says.

I was laughing at him. Honestly thinking about getting the same. What did it matter, we just had a few 22 ounce cans anyway.

"Yes we do, is Schlitz good?" The waitress asks.

"Ah yes that's perfect." Al says.

"Fuck it, cancel the ginger ale. I'll have a beer too." I say.

"Okay, 2 Schlitz, and for you?" She asks as she looks at Drew.

"Uh. I think I already said I want a ginger ale?" He responds with a bit of hesitation.

The waitress turned red and showed a nervous smile.

"Oh. Yes, of course. A ginger ale. My apologies."

"No it's fine, don't worry about it." Al says.

"Okay. Well I will be right back to you with your drinks okay guys?"

"Yes, thanks!" We all say.

We sat there talking for a minute. Al was explaining about how he did not like the whole sit down dining thing. He was always talking trash about something. He went on to explain about a time when he went into a steak house and ordered a chicken wrap. He said that when the wrap came out it was half cold and dripping with some sort of white liquid.

"Well, what did you do?" I ask.

"I sent it back dude, I'm not gonna' eat that shit, man. The waiter said it was ranch dressing but like, you don't understand. This was not ranch, dude. this was like white water that was void of any flavor at all. No way in hell was I about to eat that. Let alone pay for it in any way."

Drew is laughing his ass off as he took a swig from the beer that the waitress had just brought to our table.

"It was probably jizz bro!" Drew says, smiling.

I pause.

"Yo, shut up guys. There are kids in here eating fuckin' breakfast. The last thing their parents want to hear is the word jizz as they eat their hollandaise sauce off their eggs benedict." I say.

"Bah! You said dick'd!" Al says in a quite moronic tone.

I look at him with a look of disgust and just shake my head. The waitress approached.

"Okay, so, two English breakfasts-" she slides the plates in front of Drew and I.
"and one order of fries and a whole pickle. No salt." She says.

There was a slight pause before Al clears his throat and asks:

"Oh! Um, do you think I can get some salt?" Al asks.

She looks at him, and that pleasing smile that she presented melted away from her face faster than an ice cream cone in Death Valley.

"What the fuck!" She says.

We all lost our focus as this woman just went from completely calm to absolutely steaming mad in almost no time at all.

63

"What is your problem. You guys come in here at fuckin' 9 in the morning. Order beers, and this little prick orders some unsalted fries, so my already slammed kitchen staff has to drop all new fries, and then serve them with a fuckin' pickle, which is weird as shit by the way, just so his comedian ass can ask me for some damn salt?! Oh hell no. I am fuckin' done."

I'm not going to lie. I think I am in love with this girl. She quickly turned around and yelled towards the kitchen.

"Yo Julio, I fuckin' quit!"

Somewhere in the background I heard a baby start to cry. She took her apron and threw it at Drew and it knocked over his drink on to his plate.

"What, the fuck?!"

"Yeah, piss off." She says.

"Yo I didn't even do anything!" Drew responds.

Al was sitting with a pensive smile on his face and a slight twitch coming from his belly as he tried to hide his laughter.

"What the hell just happened?" I say as we all look at each other.

"I don't know, but that girl is a mess!" Al added.

"Al, are you serious? Your bullshit just caused this poor waitress to quit her job, how can you call her a mess. She was probably just done with it all and you put her over the edge. That's kind of messed up dude." I say to Al.

I knew it was justified because Al was lazy as hell. I don't ever remember a time when he worked. As far as anyone knew, Al just sold drugs. Well, pot, and he wasn't very good at it anyway. So I found it twisted that he thinks it is funny to mess with these honest people. A few moments of silence went by as everyone ate their food and the whole restaurant stared at us. Then drew opened his mouth again.

"So now that she is gone, who do we tip?"

Drew and I both look at him and say the same thing.

"Shut the fuck up Al."

It is then that the manager approached us in quite an angry way and says the following:

"Hello gentlemen, so it seems that one of our wait staff has just quit her job and in her leaving she mentioned that your party had said some offensive things directed at her. So we ask-"

I cut him off.
"Whoa wait. *We* said some offensive things to her?"

"That's what she said sir. Now I am going to politely ask your party to leave the restaurant. We will comp the meal and drinks but we do ask that you not return to the premises."

"Are you serious?" Al asks.

"You know what, fuck it. Guys let's just go." I say.

"Shut the hell up Al!" Drew says.

"This is your fault, douche. We were just trying to get some food and you wanted to make some sort of joke out of it."

"Such a dick." I add.

"Alright guys, let's not make this about me." Al says.

The manager cleared his throat in interruption.
"Now!" He says.

"Alright fine, we will go. But I am taking this damn beer!" I say.

"Sure. Whatever, just get out."

As we walk for the door Al yells:

"Whatever, this place sucks anyway, and the cook spit in all your food!"

I look around and see all the elderly people and middle aged folk with their children look at us with faces of disgust and anguish. Children even dropped their jaws at us. Like they had seen the devil in front of them. By god, their little minds had no idea what was in store for them. Yeah, it's all fine now. One day your eating fun shaped pancakes with your grand pappy, next thing you know, grand pappy is rotting in the earth and you are fighting with your divorced significant other about who takes the dog, the house, and child. Just wait you little brat, just wait. The hell you just witnessed would not even begin to penetrate the steel cannon ball that you call your own mind. The leather skin you call your face wouldn't bat an eyelash towards such an atrocity. But that was besides the point.

We walk over to the car and all sit down. As we sat down, Al picks up his cell phone and checks it for any notifications. He looks over it briefly and lights up with excitement.

"Holy Shit!" Drew says.

"What?" I say looking at him with a face of surprise.

He did not answer. Just kept taping the screen on his cell phone as his smile got larger. I was semi relieved to know that it was a positive subject.
"Dude, What?!" I say with legerity in my speech.

"Bro, this girl I have been seeing got tickets to the Roosters game and she has some other shit to do. She offered me the tickets!" Drew says.

"No way! How many tickets?"

"Three, dude, she gave me three free tickets!"

"Fuckin' sweet!" Al says.

The smile runs from Drew's face, as he snaps around to look at Al in the backseat. I can see in the rear view that the stupid smile on Al's face melted away as he started to judge the reaction that Al was showing. Then Al spoke.

"Dude. If you seriously think you're coming with us you're out of your fucking mind. Not after that shit you just pulled in there."

"Wait. Are you fuckin' serious?" Al says.

Drew responds with anger.

"Am I serious? Yeah I am fucking serious. You're a fuckin' child. Pulling that shit like you did. You are lucky you are even in this car right now."

"Bro you're a fuckin' asshole!" Al says with resentment in his eyes.

"Oh I am an asshole? Get out of my car." Drew responds.

"Fine!"

Al opens the door quickly and steps out. He walks away briskly as he slams the door behind him.

"Fuckin' Butthole!" Drew says.

I chuckled a bit as Drew started the car and began to drive away.

"Hey man, think you can run me to my place? Larry is there I should check on him." I ask.

Drew released a long, breathy exhale as he says:
"Yeah that's fine dude. I have to make a few phone calls too… My buddy is a huge Rooster's fan. I am going to try to find him."

"Alright, cool" I say.

We start heading home from Uptown. A semi desolate slice of town that contained a few shutdown gas stations and banks. It also contained that peach of a restaurant we were just kicked out of. I had some decent memories here. Usually the nights that had ensued after myself and a few other friends would hit the gas stations here so we could pick up cases of beer and head into the woods to party and drink our asses off. I remembered this one time a few years ago when myself and some friends decided we wanted to go up into the woods and have a fire. All was well, the fire was burning, and beers were being consumed when all of a sudden, one of the people I was with decided to go out to his truck and pull a spare car battery that was being stored in the bed and ran it into the woods like a mad man. He then, for no reason at all yelled the words,

"Battery in the fire!"

as he just slammed the lead acid battery into the fire. A swarm of red burning ash flying through the air and onto the ground as well as some of us sitting around the fire. There was a mild uproar about this before everyone extinguished the embers that were on them and ran away from the fire. The guy who did it, Roger, was kind of a speed freak and was known for doing stupid things like this. He failed to understand that it may take a little while before the battery either degassed itself or literally exploded. Needless to say, speed addicts have a notoriously short amount of patience. So that being said, Roger got the bright idea to move over closer to the battery and start poking it with a larger stick that he must have found on the floor of the woods. The rest of the group stood back as we all had the same thought.

"What an idiot." I remember hearing from one of the people standing next to me.

Everybody agreed, as we watch Roger abandon his stick by slamming it onto the burning battery and stepping towards the fire. A grimacing expression found it's way to my face as I watched Roger begin to start kicking the burning battery with his foot. I remember seeing his boot move into and out of the insufferable flames as he struck the battery. I could not believe what I was seeing. One of Roger's friends said something to him.

"Roger! Stop being stupid man, get back before that damn thing blows!"

Roger then turns around and says.

"It's not gonna' explo-"

His words were cut off by a strong release of pressurized molten lead and acid mist onto his lower back and thighs. He let out a strong sound of acknowledged severe pain as he fell forward a bit. A large plume of vaporized lead filled the air and subsequently ignited as the sulfuric acid reacted with the lead to form pure Hydrogen gas. The hydrogen then used any available oxygen around the fire, plus the added oxygen produced by the gaseous lead, and exploded with such force it knocked us all on our asses and managed to extinguish the rather large fire it was thrown into. We all blocked our face as a rain of molten metal and plastic mixed with pebbles of smoldering embers fell upon us. My ears were ringing so loud I could hardly hear my heart which felt like it had just taken a heavy-weight sized blow. I lifted my head and struggled to see a body with flames burning up its sleeves and back rolling around on the ground. I shook my head to try and comprehend what was happening and hopped to action to help Roger extinguish the flames that were still burning on him. I removed the leather jacket I was wearing and attempted to suffocate the flames. Which took longer than expected as the molten lead was so hot it was flash cooking the skin and fat on Rogers rear end. I'll never forget that smell. I swear he was crying. But I would be to, as he had 2nd and 3rd degree burns on more than %60 of his body. The back of his head was completely bald as all the hair had been burned off in the flaming boom. As I lifted my jacket off his back I saw a piece of skin come with it. So I put the jacket back down. It was his now.

I snapped back to reality.

"So, where are we going, man?" Drew asks.

"Oh just make this right and the last left at the top of the hill and I am the third and fourth house down on the left." I say.

"Alright just point out the house when we get close alright?" Drew says.

"Absolutely, no problem." I added.

We drove for a few more moments and I pointed out the house that was my home for the time being.
"That's the one." I say as I pointed to the house.

"Alright, man. I am gonna' make a few phone calls and try to find this guy."

"Alright cool." I say hastily as I exited the vehicle and headed towards the house.

I approach the house with a slight feeling of anxiety. I suppose the previous interactions with this residence have been a little rough. I arrive at the door and hear a grunting clearing of a mans throat rumble through the walls of the house. Larry must have been awake. I am sure he is not feeling the best at the moment. I grab the handle of the door. It does not twist.

"Fuck."

I attempt to turn the handle while giving the door a deep strike with the broad side of my shoulder.
It would not budge.

"Are you fucking joking?"

I can feel the neighbor looking at me in an ill fashion. I slam on the door a few times in an attempt to get Larry to come unlock it. Then I quickly realized I have no keys for this house. Probably something I should get copies of. Ah, a reason to call back the sweet looking mom of Christina.

"Larry! Larry! Open the damn door!"

In my rapping away on the wood plank of the front door I can hear the muddling of Larry clearing his throat upon waking and attempting to come to answer the door. I could not tell if he was on the first or second floor. It honestly sounded like he was banging on the ceiling in the door way. Making me even more frustrated because he was likely even closer to where I was banging on the door.

"Yo! What the hell is going on?!" Drew asks as he rolls his car window down.

I turn around to address him on the subject.

"Yeah, I'm fuckin' locked out man, I don't have a key for this door!"

"Ah, shit. Seriously? Bro, we gotta' go!" Drew says.

"Yeah man I know. Hold on." I stop speaking as I hear some movement from who I presume to be Larry inside the house.

"Ugghh." I hear echo from the home.

It was then that I heard the loud bang that sounded like a career ending fall for Larry.

"Shit!" I say as I rush down the front patio and round the corner.

I try to run up to a side window in an attempt to open it from the outside. I arrive at the first window to find it just as locked as the front door. Next window several feet up was in the same fashion. Not knowing the exact location of any of the points of egress, or in this case access. I wander around back of the house and look around. Locating a second story window that I believe I can get access too. I hope it is unlocked.

I look around, trying to locate something I could use to get my way up to the roof. There is an old large plastic cooler and a PVC lawn chair. Not exactly ideal but it would work. I grab the chair and place it on the ground near the rear wall of the house. I then put the cooler on top of it sideways and attempt to climb the contraption. It is rickety to say the least. I can hear the chair cracking as I climb the cooler. Slow and steady. I try to get up quickly and put hands on the roof. The legs were cracking harder. I get hands on the roof, and quickly lift my other leg off the chair bringing it to the top of the cooler. In one motion I attempt to bring my leg onto the roof. Success, followed by immediate failure. The leg on the flimsy PVC chair had finally buckled and collapsed. Leaving me hanging off the roof. As I am shaking off the dread of potential injury, I realize further how much of an idiot I actually am. Whatever, it was a success. Now to check the window.

Locked.

"Fuuuuck!" I say in disbelief. "Forget it, I'm breaking it."

I look around for any available item I can use to break the window. Nothing in sight. Perfect.

Then comes an idea.

I grab the belt buckle of the belt I am wearing and open the clasp, removing the belt from my waist. I step back and whip the belt buckle like a bull whip towards the center of the window. A sharp crack appears.

One more time.

A chunk of glass drops in between the two panes. Another blast. I was through the first pane. Now another. Keep whipping. Whip away the fact that your breaking and entering a home in a residential neighborhood with more drugs and illegitimate cash on the premises than could be included in one police report.

I start thinking to myself. No officer, no evidence of foul play, only a broken window where you didn't look earlier and the body of a neighborhood elderly woman in escrow to the local morgue. No sir, we don't do drugs. don't touch em'. Hopefully none of the neighbors heard me break the window.

I entered the house. What a room. Littered with mementos and pictures of younger versions of older people. The room was this awful puke green, dinged with the horrible fashions of previous decades.
Time to move on. I walked towards the door and grab the handle to exit.

"Larry!" I walk through the house yelling as I head for the stairs, to open the front door.

"Larrrryyyy!?"

Again I hear the rumbling noise from Larry. I run to his location, chasing the noise that he was making, he was upstairs. I run upstairs and continue calling him.

"Hmph." Larry lets out an agonized cry as I am approaching the location where I expect to find him. I'm there, but Larry is not.

"Larry!?" I say without haste.

"Brucie!" Larry says.

"Where the fuck are you Larry?!"

"I think I'm in the wall! Go up to the attic, the door is in the bathroom!"

"What the fuck?" I say as I go around the corner to the bathroom and locate the door up to the attic. I open the door and climb the steep stairs to the upper level. I reach the upper landing and report for Larry.

"Yo, where are ya?!" I say.

"Over here!" He responds.

I walk towards his voice and notice a large sized hole in the floor and the head and left arm of Scary Larry poking out of the orifice. I could not help but to laugh.

"What the fuck Larry? What happened?" I say, laughing.

"I frickin' came up here because I heard something up here moving around and when I came over here the dang frickin' wood broke and I fell right in."

Larry had stepped on a piece of decrepit wood and slipped into the space that must have been where a brick chimney had been dismantled at some point.

"Bruce you gotta' get me out of here man!" Larry says.

I hear Drew sound the horn on the car. I squat down to Larry and slap his head lightly.

"No can do big cat." I say. "Gotta' game to get too."

I hop up and head for the stairs.

"Brucie wait! Man you can't just leave me here! Brucie!" Larry yells.

"I'll be back later man, don't go anywhere!" I say laughing as I walk down the stairs.

I head towards the location of my drug filled microwave oven to acquire my entertainment for the night. I was feeling a bit like some speed. Drastic times call for drastic measures, and amphetamine is certainly drastic.

"White or yellow..." I say to myself as I peruse through the radioactive heating compartment.

White: Stronger. Expensive. Mellow comedown, shitty DT's.
Yellow: Cheap, Fun, more functional, shitty DT's.

I look around for a second in thought.
I'll take one of each. Deal with it all later I guess.

I can hear Drew slamming on the horn outside to get me to come out and get in the car.

"Alright, alright!" I say as I try to swallow the two speed capsules with a dry gulp.

Not an easy feat, so I dip my head into the bathroom inside and posture my head below the faucet in an attempt to get some water to assist in the ingestion of these drugs. I get some water in my mouth and swallow the mouthful before I am briskly interrupted by the insufferable honking of the damned car horn.
It startled me enough for me to strike my cheek bone against the faucet and chip one of my molars.

"Fuck!" I say while I check the area for signs of bleeding.

"Alright I'm coming!" I yell, as I head for the door in a hurry. I can hear Larry speak in a muffled tone through the layers of sheet rock and stucco.

"Brucie wait man, please don't leave me here I am freaking out!" He proclaims.

"Just go to sleep Lar' I will be back soonish!" I yell back.

I can honestly say I felt sort of bad in a way but what the hell I wouldn't be able to get him out anyway. I exit the house and slam the door without realizing it. No way are these amphetamines kicking in yet. Must have just been fired up at the moment. I walk towards the car with a hustle, only to have a close call with a passing SUV that would have probably liquefied me.

"Watch where your going ya' fuckin' gimp!" I yell at the passing car in an attempt justify my lack of attention.

I can see Drew smirk at me as I run across to the passenger door of his car so I can climb in.

"Everything alright?" Drew asks.

"Yeah man, besides almost getting broadsided by that fucking elephant on wheels and Larry being lodged in the walls of my current living situation, I am fine. Oh and chipping my tooth on a faucet while trying too-" I clear my throat. "get a drink." I continue.

Drew laughs.

"Well I am sorry man." He says as we pull away from the road.
"Good news though, I got a hold of my buddy Greg. We gotta' go pick him up from the bowling alley."
"Alright cool, sounds good. What? Does this guy work over there?"

"No, the dude lives over there." He responds.

I give Drew a look and we head on our way, but just barely. Drew has this car, it is a little older but he has this impressive sound system in it with these giant woofers that would shake every damn bolt and panel on the car. He would constantly have to readjust his rear view mirror because it would constantly become misdirected due to the unbelievable vibration. He turned up the levels on this electronic dance song that he had loaded in the CD deck. I felt the bass rattle my sinuses and had to turn it down.

"Damn Drew, chill with that. It's too damn loud man!" I say.

He laughs

"Alright, alright. My bad." He says.

Off we went.

Over the next few moments, I could not have seen what was coming. The amphetamines and subconscious concern for my own life must have triggered one of the strongest feelings of anxiety I have ever felt. Such degradation. Who the fuck am I, why am I here. Why the fuck is any of this here. Why can life be so fucking cruel to those who don't deserve such cruelty and so rewarding to those who deserve absolutely nothing. Damn. A cold winter. A hot summer. A calm fall. A living spring. I could feel a tear form in my eye and that burning sensation in my nose. No. Not this. You are a glimpse of a sub par species in an ever rotting and degrading universe. Entropy in its finest. Such potential. Such inconceivable fucking torture with such little gratitude just meandering through this life like the all knowing powers that be, want us to do. Before the cold of winter destroys us. The pain is immense. The heat of summer entraps us. Pulls out the inside emotion. The fall reminds of the calm before such great death. The spring engulfs us. Reminds us of life and instills a fleeing bit of hope. It is no wonder humans have deity's. I just cannot imagine how difficult it must have been for the first humans to convince themselves of such a thing. Calm down Bruce. Don't have an episode. Don't do this to Drew, or even yourself. Stay positive. Stay without care. You're on drugs.

We arrive at the bowling alley, and just as I remembered, there are no houses or apartments near the bowling alley. Drew parks the car and steps out. I get out after him and follow.

The bowling alley was closed, what the hell was going on here? Drew looks around as he walks quickly towards the rear of the building and spots a piece of ply wood covering a crawl space entrance near the rear of the building.

He knocks on it. Which I found ironic in a way because it just fell down. Privacy respected by human, disregarded by physics. Unbelievable.

       I hear a grunt and a cough followed by:
"Yo!"

       "Yo Greg what's up man, I got my buddy Brucie with me." Drew asks.

       "That's cool, you guys ready to head in? When does the game start?" Greg says.

       "Tip off is at 7 P.M. so we have a little bit of time. I figure we can head in now and catch a beer or something." Drew says this with an almost insinuating tone.

       "Oh, no man. I am actually sober now Drew, for once and for all. I had to do something, ya' know? So, yeah, no beer for me. Sorry guys."

       Oh, that makes sense. Drew must be testing him. This guy has no idea what he is getting into.

       "Yeah that's cool man no worries! Right Brucie, that shouldn't be a problem, right man?" Drew asks, subtlety forcing me to agree with him.

       "Yeah, yeah that's fine man, no worries at all." I respond.

       "Alright cool, well we can get some grub than, let's roll." Drew says as he heads for the exit.

       We walk towards the car and got in. Greg got in the backseat and started yawning as he spoke.

       "I gotta' get the fuck out of here man. This place is terrible. I can't fucking sleep."

       I couldn't help but react to the things he was saying. Is this guy serious? He lives underneath a fucking bowling alley. He went on.

       "I fuckin' hate bowling man. I really do. Every time I try to fall asleep I get woke up by the loud banging of those damn bowling balls smacking the fucking ground."

       Drew and I both start laughing.

       "I was sleeping when y'all came in. The only time I can get any sleep is after 3 a.m. when this hell hole closes."

I laugh.

"Well dude you can knock out for a little bit. We have a two hour drive and if you want you can get some sleep." Drew s.

Drew was in a nice mood now.

"Yo, thank you Drew, and thanks for inviting me to come. I almost didn't answer the phone when you called. My employment advisor that the state appointed me has been ringing me up the fucking wall. They give you this phone to get on your feet and just ring you non stop all day with offers to work next to other criminals."

"Rough." I say in response.

"Right? I don't know, it could be worse. At least I am staying sober." Greg adds.

"Yeah man! How long has it been?" Drew asks.

"Well about 2 weeks now. Never felt better. My head is clear, it feels great!"

I love hearing the sober tales of people. They are so adamant that they had a problem. I mean seriously, be modest. Everyone likes drugs of some sort. You, on the other hand, may have liked them just a little bit more.

"That is great, Greg. Excellent." Drew says.

At this time I am wondering, How long has he been out of jail. Or rather the program that which resulted in him having basically a parole officer. Furthermore, how bad was this problem. Mainly so I can meter my own use.

"I feel great!" Greg yelled, in a very intense, alarming fashion.

"Whoa, well alright!" I say slightly startled.

I made a move towards the button to roll down the windows. His energy was absolutely making me uncomfortable. Likely do to the strange mushy feeling the drugs are causing me. Which in itself was also strange. One of those must not have been speed. But what could it be?

"Alright so where are we heading?" Greg asks

"Like I said, we have about a two hour ride into the city buddy. Then we have to get to McCormin Stadium." Drew responds.

"Ah perfect," Greg says, "yeah I think I am just gonna' pass out for a bit than."

Excellent.

"Alright dude." Drew says.

So here I am. On the verge of a mental collapse. It must not have been speed that I took. I mean the pill was not necessarily in any type of distinctly marked bottle. Damn, it could have been Cyanide for all I know. Maybe scopolamine. Maybe some sort of downer. At least that is what it felt like. I could be dying. But I guess we all are. No big deal. Every few minutes I am experiencing a bolt of clarity. Likely the amphetamines battling it out. I can say confidently that *one of them must* have been amphetamines. My goodness this was a mistake and a half. Think Bruce think! What could I actually get my hands on. Maybe some sort of opiate? Well that can't be, I am slightly allergic to opiates. I would be itching like I rolled in fiberglass insulation. It feels more chemical. Like maybe benzo's but not so calming. More, disassociating. Maybe GHB? It could be. Easy to make, Easily acquirable. I think that was it. It felt familiar. My goodness, there is GHB in Smog Town? That is scary actually. This drug is familiar among sexual predators and malicious drug users. The people that would buy another person a drink and spike it to take advantage of them when the GHB takes hold. Not the type to drug you and your significant other take on the day of your celebration, though some people do party with it. People who use GHB likely only do so to take advantage of the situation. From ravers to rapists, there will always be good ol' GHB. This was likely a dose to drop the average sized early 20's female. But not a full grown Brucie. Time will heal all wounds. Just got to hang tough. Music! Play some music!

"Hey can we play some music?" I ask to Drew.

"Yeah man, turn on the radio. But try to keep it low I think Greg is asleep." He replies.

I moved my hand to the head unit in the car and attempted to turn it on. I'll be honest I wasn't really positive which button did it so I just pressed the preset selection button to which nothing happened in response. Obviously not the damn button.

"Ah, I don't know how to start this fuckin' thing." I say in subtle anger.

Drew laughs and spoke in humor:

"I'll do it man."

He reaches his hand over to push the power button, and pushes it. A bright flash lights up the stereo and immediately ceases.

Damn. That was my last hope.

"Damn it! The fucking fuse must of blown again."

This was perfect. I really was not sure if I could handle silence at this time. It was unbearable. I was not in the mood to talk. I was tapped out of conversation and had a fear that if I kept motioning towards conversation I would likely just be posing a fake smile and nodding my head to the rhythm of agreement with whatever the hell Drew was saying. He could be preaching antisemitism, and strictly to satisfy my unbelievable hunger for continuing satisfaction in the wake of my rampant drug use, I would agree completely. I was the ideal form. I picture some sort of all knowing all judging deity resting in his loft in the clouds looking down on me, lowering his trendy sunglasses, and smiling in approval. Such an angel I am. I start to smell something rancid creep from the back seat. Like a mixture of sauerkraut and burnt matches.

"Oh g'damn! That is terrible." I say, darting my hand for the switch to roll the window down to vent the hot stink.

Greg was foul. Unbelievable. Whatever, maybe I will just clock out too, or at least close my eyes.

"Hey, I am gonna' get some shut eye for a little while, is that cool?" I ask Drew.

"Yeah it's fine man." he responds.

What little sleep I got, closing my eyes in an effort to gain some sort of sanctuary failed miserably. I sat there thinking about my past, and in the worst way. I could see myself as a young man. The issue of my almost successful existence. Oh, the things I would say to my early 20's self. The context in which our generation was being perceived was unbelievable. People calling my generation lazy, and entitled. I was working two jobs, struggling to make rent and have the ability to eat anything besides dollar store chicken nuggets and pot pies, 2 for the price of 1. Struggling was just your way of life. Everyone was eating shit. Everyone was struggling, so it just seemed normal. But not to a soul like mine. A soul like mine was offended directly by this atrocity of a comment made upon my generation. I listened to this forty-something year old man outside a local pub and remember not even having the guts to stand up for myself, or my generation, as he loudly called people my age "horrible." I remember hearing this and just lowering my head and walking away. Just like a beaten down nail who isn't ready to be hammered yet. I stood up right with a crooked neck and lowered head. My pride holding me rigid like the steel, my ego bent crooked. Also, so inquisitive toward the virtue of nails, this particular nail was the proverbial, "last nail in the coffin" of my, at the time, monetary situation. After that comment, I changed. I went towards the goal. I grew a pair of balls and grabbed the world by the horns. I went out and got a sales job.

I laugh under my breath. Drew looks over at me and asks in a comical tone:

"You okay, Brucie?"

"Yeah, just a funny thought." I respond, followed by an awkward silence.

Drew went back to driving, as I went back to thinking. It was actually calming me down.

I took a better job. I wanted it so bad. I wanted to not have to struggle anymore. I wanted life. I wanted to have my bills paid and be able to afford the nicer things. But instead of wants, one thing I needed, was happiness. I was so unhappy. Needless to say, I did well. I remember after I had saved my first real bit of money how good it felt to be able to go out to that same pub and pay for drinks and food for myself and my lady friend for that evening. Being casually unworried for any unforeseen event. Escorting this dame outside with my new trendy clothes on and her luxurious Friday night attire. I must look more dolled up than she did.

My goodness. Was that really me?

I take her hand and open the passenger side door as I guide her into the passenger seat of my sporty yet conventional saloon style car. We laugh, and speed off. Destination set to be my 3 star apartment on the edge of town. It was quaint. A loft style apartment but furnished well with plenty of shiny things and lightly colored wood textures. All laminate of course. The place was cheap. It just looked good. Most of the girls I escorted to this place liked it. Thinking back, I liked it as well. I miss it. What a life I could have lived had I not been so damn bored.

So where did I go wrong?

I got very bored of it all. I can not explain why but in regards to the way I was living I got so sick of looking at the same things over, and over, and over. The same people at the same damn pub talking about the same damn thing. I felt awfully lavish. I remember looking down on someone who was the same age as me and thinking nothing of it. What had I become. By that time I had made my fair share of money. The company I had joined had been picked up under a franchising agreement and the owner, who had recognized my hard efforts toward this business, offered me a percentage of the buyout. I was sitting pretty. Pretty enough to not need to work. To be honest though in retrospect I really should have stayed in a working environment. I invested about half of the money, and lived off the other, and all was fine. Even thinking about what happened next made my nose start to sting and my eyes water. I didn't ever want to be there again. Looking back on it was difficult.

The breakdown.

I suffered a long coming breakdown of my mind and well being. I simply woke up one morning in a panic. What was I doing? Why was I here, why was I alone? Why the fuck did I care? After dozens of doctor visits and hours of therapy sessions, I had my answer. It laid in the bottom of bottle of booze. Drugs reentered my life much like an industrial wrecking ball into a decrepit building. Before you knew it. I was dissecting 'poo-poo' roaches to smoke out of an empty beer can. Now a days I can confidently say I have *spilled* more drugs than most people will do in an entire life time.

That doesn't bother me though. The way life chewed me up didn't bother me either. I largely blamed myself. Who else was to blame? I had a shot and lost focus and fell so hard it must have made a crater so big that I could never climb out. I don't care. I don't care about any of this.

I felt some solace in those words. 'I don't care.' I guess it meant something to me. As screwed up as it may be.

My mind wandered no more, I took deep breaths until I fell asleep.

I don't usually dream if I am on speed, but then again, I don't usually sleep on speed at all. Unless it is meth, meth makes me sleepy. So maybe there was some meth in the mix. The GHB must have stronghold on the speed. But the speed must be making my mind go hyper. My dream was intense, but familiar. It was dark, almost too dark to see, a blue tone to the surroundings from a moon reflecting light back to the ground. A group of people are beside me, all in good spirits. All familiar faces from friends and lovers I have known in my life. They were smiling. But I knew something was wrong. Unsure of this feeling I got up from the log I was sitting on. We were all collected behind a barn. With a grassy embankment behind us, and the long side of the barn in front. I ran to the front of the barn to see a large yellow fireball hurdling down from the sky. It was massive. A giant yellow sphere with the most beautiful shimmering fire trail behind it. I felt immediate panic as I looked around to see that everybody I was with was not alarmed by this sight. They didn't care. I was quickly humbled by this, and went back to get a good spot to see this somniferous meteor drive itself into the planet. As it became critically close I was closer to the group, as we were all now watching together. I closed my eyes and said out loud:

"I love you all."

A moment of silence before the blast made me open them. I watched the wall of the blast approach me quickly and without quarter of any kind. It moved quickly. Blasting me awake. I jumped in my seat.

Stretching immediately after I am startled awake, I release a long yawning growl.

"You alright?" Drew asks.

"Yeah I'm good. Where are we?"

"Just got here." Drew says.

"Fuckin' sweet!" I yelled. Throwing back my hand to wake up the guy in the back seat. I am greeted with another long growling yawn from him.

"Hey bone-boy get up! We are here!" I yell at him.

He laughs as he says, "alright, alright!"

We roll out of that car like we were 50 pound bags of shit. All greasy and looking like the day or week before. Such a colorful city it is. So ethnic and enriched in its own heritage. Everyone bustling about as if they had somewhere to truly be. Didn't any of them understand that this was all a joke? I mean where are you all going anyway, to work? Work is for suckers. Following the pack deprives the world of leaders. Remember that.

I took a tingly legged step towards the venue and nearly ran into an Asian toddler. His mother scooped him away and I swear she hissed at me. Maybe it was the drugs. Who knows, I just go where the wind blows. This struck me as profound for some reason. I'd heard that before. But where? I must have been a little snot nosed kid because for some reason it reminded me of childhood. No, the child reminded me of childhood. Or maybe it was both. I don't know. I am hardly even alive right now.

Drew bumped into me, His words breaking my pause.

"Brucie! What the fuck are you doing?"

"Nothing!" I say, as I pushed him back.

At that exact moment, some random older gentleman, with diamond studs in his ears grabs my shoulder and says:
"What are you doing out here?! They let you out?!"

Needless to say I was puzzled deeply by this action. Greg and Drew both look at each other puzzled.
I smile at the man and say:

"Sir, I have no idea what the hell your talking about."

He fires back a look at me like I stole his lollipop and asks "Aren't you Dave's kid?"

A fairly long pause passed before I let out a slightly extended, "…No."

"OH! Well ya' look just like him!" He says.

"Alright?" I say with a slight smile as he scurries away.

"What the fuck was that?" Drew asks.

"I have not the slightest damn clue what that was." I say.

I shook my head a bit. That rubbed me the wrong way. It was very weird. Again reminding me of my childhood for some strange reason.

"Well let's go man we might be late."

"Alright."
We walk.

What a scene it was. How unbelievable I felt. Like a plane crashing, but if the plane was flying underwater. It had rained a bit on the ride in. Making all the unprepared attendees soaked in precipitation from their one to one-hundred block walk to the stadium. This made me uncomfortable. It brought back deep feelings of discomfort and neglect for myself. A time when I was hanging out in a small bar back in smog town. It was mid February and we had just had a large snowfall so the roads and sidewalks were coated in a salty, wet mess that would easily be tracked into the building by the feet of the loyal patrons. It was a Thursday night. I remember because the true patrons would get their head start on the weekend by going out the night before the weekend as well. No shame in that. I didn't have a damn job. I was coasting of a little scheme Larry and I devised in which we would wake up early and beat the lines to the free pantry and sell the food to the hoodlums at the park for a few bucks. Larry once sold half a bottle of chartreuse to a kid down there for sixty bucks. It was especially impressive because he bartered up from an expired bag of frosted donuts that he traded to an elder woman. I was impressed with Larry.

Larry and I were sitting at the end of the bar. Enjoying our Long Island iced teas made only with the finest well grade liquor. It was the most amazing sight. As the night fell closer into the late hours the patrons would get drunker, and drunker, and drunker. Of course, due to the weather outside, and the frequent trips outside to smoke cigarettes and sneak bumps of shitty coke, the inside floor was becoming very wet, and very slippery. As the 6th or 7th replay of the same damn songs came on the jukebox, their would decay and they would dance worse, and worse. Before long, you were watching people slide across the floor and take nasty spills over and over onto an unkempt floor. Seeing pretty girls in their white jackets get covered in salty brown stains as they tried to navigate the indoor ice rink with humps and heels on. The bartender just smiling. Feeding drinks to them. Watching them fall. Larry and I were disturbed by this. We stopped going to bars after that. I guess the discomfort just changed us. From that point on, we were day drinking, whenever and wherever we wanted to. Screw the bar.

I was getting that same discomfort *here*. The gross floor and all the people all soaked with runny noses. Smokers, smelling like a wet, half smoked cigarette. I don't know why I was bitching though. Honestly, I could've used a walk in the rain. I am sure I smell terrible. That is next on the list. Take a shower in the dead lady's house, and save Larry. Should probably help Larry first.

As we approached the seating decks there are vendors selling draft beers and various premixed drinks. I see Greg give one of them a look not unlike that of a hungry lion with a helpless zebra in its path. I hope he wasn't thinking what I thought he was thinking. Because if he is thinking what he thought when I am now thinking it, than it's a thought. Not a good thought, but a bad thought. It looks like I am going to have to keep an eye on this one. A, 'half faded off of some mystery substance and burnt-out "eye". An, over served drunk searching for an '18' on the dartboard with one eye opened, type "eye."

Drew is leading. He had the ticket in his grasp and was on a mission, which was good because I am essentially useless at this point. I would likely sleep through this game, or not. It really depends on what the chemicals want to do. I am more or less along for the ride at this point. Where is this strange man taking me. 'Man' being some off-white powder we kept in the microwave. Such profound thought.

We arrive at our seats, but not shortly after tripping over the steep and somewhat non drunk friendly steps of the stadium bleachers. Sadly, to my own, discovery we were sat next to a somewhat perfect family.

The Father:
>The remnants of a man. His eyes screamed of agonizing discontent with himself and his world. I can remember his type. He likely spends his lunch break in the seedy fluorescent lit rooms behind the thin walls of a corporate world. With a group of other miserable I.D. badge humans acting enthusiastic about how their little ones always lose their name brand socks. Sliding his bulbous ass into a pair of balloon wasted khaki pants. Tucking in the pinstripe button up and sliding his name badge over his bald head.
His smile reeks a stench of guilt. Misplaced of course. It resembled as if a something was inside him, crying to come out. Reminiscent of a pawn, in a much larger corporate game.

The Mother:
>Absent, yet futile. Invisible to another man. Her brows perfectly groomed. Her hair is obviously important to her. Visually shameless to anyone but herself. Needlessly bullying the kids into any position she wants them to be in. Clearly a menace to anyone beside her. Likely gets a new minivan every year. This woman is a terror. I could *smell* the way she looked at us as we neared the seats designated for us. Because of course, they were adjacent to their two children.

Child 1:
Obviously Older. Slightly vacant. Just happy to not be in bed.
Child 2:
Obviously younger. Not terribly behaved, but definitely impressionable.

I observe their seating and immediately position myself to not be the one sitting next to the children. I take a lot of shots at people, but I don't mess with kids. You never know with kids these day.   Shit, I mean one could have a gun and bad intentions.
Drew is going in first. Perfect. He won't potentially traumatize the kids like my insufferable drug use most certainly will. I am sure we are quite something to look at. Except Drew, He was somewhat normal. So it's good he was the first point of contact. Drew hangs out with a two homeless dudes though, so he is no gem. I wish Larry was here. He would have been fun. We took our seats and began to talk shit over the loud voices around us. I started to feel a little goofy and began toying with Drew by using some sparring word with antagonizing tone.

"So Drew, Whats up? Did you take you diarrhea med's?"

"Brucie! Shut the fuck up, man!."

He is such a douche.
"Well damn! Sorry man, I am just looking out for you. I know your

hemorrhoids are bothering you."

He was turning red.

"Yeah, Brucie. You really need to take it easy when you eat my ass! You're giving me some pretty bad piles!"

I burst out laughing so hard it projectiles a little bit of spit out of my mouth and into the hair of a curly haired woman sitting in the row below us and on to Greg's dirty ass pants. He began laughing as well.
Drew got me. It made me feel better.

The lights went down as some music began to play and a deep toned man began announcing the teams coming in. His voice screamed over the intercom:

"Ladies and Gentlemen! Please, put your hands together for the Metropolitan Roosters!"

The crowd proceeded to go wild at the demand of this random deep voiced man, I was strangely intrigued by this in my current mental state. I look over to Greg and Drew, who are cheering and clapping rather violently. I was now uncomfortable. Looking down at the court I see the roster of players start exiting the tunnel below the bleachers, which I can only assume is a tunnel to some sort of mystical semi-satanist wonderland full of hedonism and shameless vice. One can only wonder.

The announcers voice continued:

"And Now… Our visiting team! With a record of 17 and 1, the current two time running U.S. Pro Series Champions, The Diceburg… COUGARS!"

This announcer is clearly in favor of the visiting team. I thought this seems odd. As I watch the visiting team exit the magic tunnel, it seemed like each and every one of them was crouching or posturing in a certain way just to fit through the walls.

"Good god…" I mumble.

It echos over a dead audience as these behemoths captured the attention in a tone of discontent for their home and favorite team. They are going to get destroyed. Everyone knew this. I look over at Greg and Drew, whose enthusiasm has escaped them. For some reason this amuses me. I guess my lack of care for this sport allowed me to observe this ridiculous spectacle as nothing more than another win in the clearly better teams record. The announcer said seventeen and one! Holy shit, who beat these giants?

In the first 5 minutes of this game. Five players were injured and out of the game with subs in before the end of the first period. It was a Horror show. I look over to Drew, who was now slouched in his seat with a single hand covering half his face. That's not good. That's how you get pimples.

"I'm gonna' go take a piss." I heard Greg say reluctantly as he got up and walked away.

I respond with a simple, "alright."

"Drew… What's up man? You okay?"

He postured up and took his hand of his face and says:
"Yeah man. I don't know. I just feel kinda' stupid for not looking into these tickets before accepting them, but like, what are you gonna' do, ya' know?"

I began to laugh.
"Why is that? Do you think your friend gave you these tickets so she wouldn't have to see her favorite team get demolished by basically the nuclear warhead of sports teams?"

He looks at me with a scolding insulted look and says:

"Yeah, Brucie. That's what I think."

I laugh a little.

"Well, don't worry about it dude, let's just enjoy the game." I say.

Easy for me to say, I'm high as a kite.

"Yeah, I know man, I'm just bummed out."

Obviously I could see that already.

"Well chill man, just watch a little longer and let's see, maybe they can make a comeback."

He looks at me and laughs a bit.
"I don't think so bro."

We both laugh. I feel I may have helped. But really, only did so to be able to watch this show go on, and with a score of 36 to 4 in the first I don't think any comebacks will be occurring. Guess we can just watch the game now.
By the middle of the 2nd period the home team was whooped. The

score was 87 to 15. The home team's coach was sitting with his arm's crossed. He had nothing left. All of his tricks, nothing was working. It was quite sad, yet interesting. The crowd sure had thinned out. With only a few Roosters fan battling to fight a numerous flock of Cougars fans screaming at every point scored.

It was then that Greg came back. A bit too smiley if you ask me, But he came back.

He seemed different. Maybe a bit tense. Perhaps something happened in the bathroom he isn't too comfortable with. Like maybe someone looked at his wiener, made a comment, you know. The usual.

"Hey! What's going on Greg, back from your shit?"

The family looks at me angrily.

"Uh, yeah… It went, well." He says.

"Well, that's good! Good for you!"

Who says their shit went well. It seemed a little too casual. Something was up with him, and I was going to find out. What could it be? How do I find out without being too forward. Should I just say screw it and ask him what's going on? No, can't do that.

"So what did I miss?" Greg asks.

"Not much, Roosters are getting destroyed out here. The referee must be drunk, and I'm fuckin' hungry!" Drew says, being quite hostile.

The family started to pack up their stuff. I noticed that the mother was doing so extra ferociously. I couldn't just let this aggression go under the radar.

"Excuse me ma'am, is something wrong?"

She did not see this coming at all. The shock took over her face like nothing else. She was forced to tell the truth, and as much as it conflicted with her strong values, she was ready to be honest.

"Look me and my friends are a bunch of fuckin' assholes. Don't mind us, we are just bullshitting. Personally I am high as balls right now and really shouldn't be here. But hey, public forum, am I right?! God Bless America!"

I think she was ready to explode.

While this conversation was going on Drew and Greg were hot on the trail of making a good point. Drew was explaining a situation in which he noticed that every time the Cougars scored a point, the referee would briefly turn to his left and scratch his crotch, which was a lot. They got to theorizing that the referees ball bag must have been bloody raw at this point. Which has lead to much speculation. I had noticed that the children of the woman I was speaking with are rather intrigued by this conversation and decided to look for themselves. The father looks about ready to hit Drew. But he knew the implications of which. How would he explain it to his precious children? Violence really *is* the answer?

The mother snapped back.

"I have NEVER, seen someone as disgusting and pathetic as you!"

Oh damn, easy ma'am, You're revving me up with those insults.

"How dare you, come to a public place like this, high off your ass and stinking like… like, like- FUCKING TRASH!"

The children gasped.

"Mommy?" they both say.

The husband reached his hand out and puts it on his wife's shoulder.

"Susan, Sto-"

"No!" she interrupted.

Oh, things are getting good. Drew and Greg stopped their magnificent theory of the eternal itch so they could observe the awakening of the devil inside this woman.

"No, Gary! These *LOSERS* have played with our kindness for the last time and I have had enough! I'm going to tell these piece of shit, loser, freaks and their drug addict, douche bag, butt buddy to get lost! And that the only good they could do to the world would be going home and running into a knife, because they are better off dead, than in here polluting the world with their filth… Now kids, grab your things, we are leaving this idiot fest and heading home."

The husband's jaw had to be picked up off the floor before he stuttered to even comprehend what just happened. The kids are laughing and cheering for their mother. I see the look in her husbands eyes as she commanded her way out of the scenario. They are the lustful eyes, the ones that scream "damn Susan, let's go put the kids to bed, and make another one in the back of the minivan." I applaud this man, and his strangely sexy wife.

      We were so blown away by what just happened. Our immediate reaction was to laugh at each other, But then it occurred to us that this women made the whole night reach a climax. We had no choice, but to start clapping.

      The clapping caught the attention of the surrounding attendees who had heard this debacle. They must have found it worthy of applause as well. The cheers eventually caught the attention of all of those around and before long, the other side of the court was cheering. Even the teams had noticed the cheering and all paused to see what was happening. They had no idea what they are cheering for, but sheep will be sheep. At this point the family had gathered their things and started leaving the arena, and I have never felt more loved. What a woman, I think I am in love.

      All this excitement has me on edge. Enough so, to notice that Greg was seeming a bit more giddy than before. He had also started burping quite often. Now I don't know about you, but I know a drunk when I see one, and this dude was drunk. This was a big deal. He was in recovery. Not a big deal to me, but to someone. Do I rat the man out, or do we end up hanging out. I think he might suspect I know based on how I am looking at him. Or maybe he thought I was trying to hook up with him. I really don't know, I was pretty high myself.

      A few minutes later, the last buzzer rang and signaled the end of the game. Final score, 128 to 34. A true slaughtering. Now we fully understood why the tickets were free.

      "So what now, should we hit a bar?" I ask.

      "Well, as long as Greg is okay with hanging out at the bar and not drinking, I would be down to go to the bar." Drew says.

      I didn't expect Greg to want to go to a bar and not have a few drinks, because honestly who the hell wants to go to a bar and not drink. Why would you ever want to go to a damn bar and not drink. So you can spend four bucks on a soda-pop and try to talk over every loud mouth hag that's in there trying to bitch about their life to a prospective hook up.

      "Sure, I'll go!" Greg says.

      Well, I guess I am wrong. But in a way this supports my suspicion. This guy is drunk or on drugs.
Trust me, I'm a professional.

After fussing and fighting among the disappointed crowd we hit the road so hard I think I felt the aftershock. When we arrive at the bar several minutes later. I started to feel achy and irritable. Could have been the drugs I suppose. I really need to stop that shit. The doing drugs and all. I think I could be a much better person if I gave them up. But until then, looks like I am going to be high most the time.

As we walk through the narrow doors to this shady dive bar we are greeted to a fairly busy situation. Not unlike the entrance to the stadium, it was sopping wet and cold. Made for a very uncomfortable bar in my opinion, but none of the patrons seemed to care. I guess I'll just harness their energy for a bit. As we rounded the last three seats open at the bar I see four professional looking business men take notice that we are taking the seats. The men cursed among themselves and stormed out of the bar. This would be the first patrons we would cost the bar, but certainly not the last. It gave me a bit of cold inspiration. Let's just be as nasty and inconsiderate as possible. This way, we can maybe get this bar emptied out and I would feel comfortable again. Sounds like a plan. What can I do?

Well, my shoes are wet. First things first, lets get these bad boys taken off and warm my wet socks up on the brass bar that ran across the bottom of the bar. My goodness my feet are stinky. I suppose that happens when you wear the same shoes for a few days straight after floating through sea foam and salt water. I don't think I had even taken my shoes off since then. As a matter of fact, the rain water was likely doing the shoes good at this point to wash out all that awful smelling foot odor and mildew. My goodness did they stink. Even to me, and not to long ago I was squatting in a basement with a guy who eats food from dumpsters. I could see the people across the bar and the looks on their face go from happy-go-lucky, to as if someone had just spit in their face. One or two immediately call to close out their tab. It was working perfectly.

"Holy shit, Brucie. Are those your fucking feet that smell that bad?" Drew asks.

"Oh, uh. Yeah. I guess so." I respond.

"Good lord put your fucking shoes back on you dirty motherfucker, your feet smell like a dead hookers ass." Drew says out loud.

How very rude. It seemed as if his comment is met with further disgust among the other patrons surrounding our group. Greg was clearly uncomfortable.

I wonder to myself how Larry was doing.

"Look dick nose, my feet are ice cold and wetter than your mother. Now, chill out on the comments you're hurting my feelings, yeah?" I for some reason say the end of that statement in a British accent.

Greg chuckled.

"Okay, well look Brucie, no offense man, but your feet do fuckin' reek." Greg says.

I look at them both sparingly and observe the rest of the bar. They all are looking at us. The bartender as well. I guess I have to make a choice.

"Fuck. Well fine than!"

I stood up from my bar stool.

"If anyone steals this seat, I'll rub my fuckin' toes on your shirt." It was a really empty insult. Really more comical than anything, by the way the bar was reacting to it.

I stand up and make my way towards the door. The bartender looking at my feet pensively as he didn't even want to see those socks touching his floor. Even though the floor was already filthy from foot traffic.

As I got to the door, I swung it open with one hand. I lift up each foot and slowly peeled the withering cotton science experiments from my feet and pulled them off. First the left foot, then the right. Just like always. I took the socks, and with the door open, just hurdle them out the door with little regard for the possible bio-hazard I just introduced into the local ecosystem. I think they might of hit someone walking on the street, but I didn't stick around to look.

The door slammed shut.

I walk back to my stool barefoot and through the swamp of wet waste water dragged in from the city street. Surely a fresh drink of water to these things. The bar tender handed me a plastic bag to put my shoes in while we are there.

"Excellent, thanks man." I say while shoving the bag down by my feet, totally disregarding his gesture and sliding my dirty feet into my shoe bare foot.

"So what will it be boys" He says.

"Well-" I glance at his name tag.

"Nancy?!"

Why was this man named Nancy. I chuckled a little. Drew noticed this as well and smirked a bit. The bartender rolled his eyes and it seemed he had likely gotten a lot of crap about his name his whole life.

Better not stoke the fire.

"Uh, I'll have a rum and coke." I say, quickly looking over to Drew.

"Yeah, I suppose I'll just have a Schlitz." He says.

So now it was up to Greg. We both sat there looking at him, positioned on his left, and on his right. See, I have my suspicion that he is already drinking. So I am expecting him to order a drink. But Drew, who knew he was some time sober, was excited to see him order a non-alcoholic beverage. The pressure was mounting.

"Uh- Uh I'll have, a cranberry juice."

Damn, Maybe I am wrong. Maybe it's me who is screwed up. But he did sound a bit reluctant.

"Ya' know, for a second there, I thought you were gonna' order a beer!" Drew says.

"How long has it been now?" He asks.

"I don't know... couple months." Greg answers.

"Oh?" Drew replied.
 It seemed as if there was a bit of disbelief in his tone and I could feel this as well. He was up to something. It was obvious now. I mean, just a few moments ago he was saying it was only a couple weeks of sobriety. Drew looks over to me quickly, and quickly looks away. Scanning the room until he spots a credit card operated jukebox on the wall.

"Hey Brucie, You wanna' go pick a song on the jukebox?"

"Uh. Not really dude. I mean, I have no-" I blurt, before he interrupts,

"Oh come on lets go pick something."

I could tell he was trying to do something. But I didn't really care.

"Bro, I have no fuckin' shoes-"

He interrupts me again,

"Brucie! I want to see if they have that song, come on man!" He says.

"Fuck, aright fine!" I get up and follow him to avoid what feels like a public outcry about my feet again.

As we are walking over I start to grief about my feet again.
"Look dude, I know they fucking smell give me a break I haven't gotten to go grab a new pair-"
He interrupts a third time.

"I'm not pulling you over here to talk about your feet, douche. Look, did you give anything to him? Because he's acting fucked up and he has been sober for a little bit now and I swear if you fucked that-" I interrupt him.

"What? No dude. I was actually thinking the same thing. It was like after he went to the bathroom he came back all weird and wiggly." I say.

"Wiggly? Okay Brucie, I don't really know what the fuck that means, but yeah. I agree. He is certainly acting a bit different. You swear you didn't give him anything?" Drew asks.

"I swear dude." I reply.

"Alright." He says, reluctantly. "But if you see him do anything, call him out, or like tell me or something. To be honest I can believe it if he did. I mean seriously, do I need to fucking watch him piss now too? Can't trust a junkie dammit."

"Yeah dude, no problem, I'll absolutely let you know. But I am going to get back to the bar because I don't trust him to be alone like this."

"Yeah, good idea." Drew says as he swipes his card in the jukebox.

I walk back to the bar to see that our drinks have arrived and it appears that our cups are a little less full than the top of the glass. Maybe I was just mistaken. I shrugged that one off. His cranberry juice however, did seem a bit different in color than I would expect. I sat down, and take a sip of my drink. Which is actually put together really well.

"Mm.. That's good."
I see the bartender looking over and I signal him a thumbs up, to which he seemed sort of shocked. Damn. Did he do something to this drink? Blood sucking savage. Was it the Nancy thing? I hope not. Damn it, it also looks like

boozy here skimmed some of our drinks. I see the bartender look away in a concerned way and walk out from behind the bar, and walk over to Greg. I quickly look over to Greg. My eyes watch cautiously, better not look obvious.

"So how's that juice, my friend?" I ask

"Huh? Oh, yeah it is pretty cool. I mean good- It's pretty good." Greg answers.

"Oh yeah? That's good, that's good."

I start to gaze out across the bar over the patrons to see Drew wrapping up his conversation with the bartender. They seem jolly. Not a bad confrontation from my observation. However, Drew is moving quite fast. I lock eyes with him and he stops. He puts on this urgent face and gestures me to come over to him. Fair enough.

"Hey listen Greg, I am gonna' go see if I can bum a smoke off of one of these fools." I say as I stand up and make my way towards Drew.

Greg was watching the recap on TV to the game we all had just come from.

"Okay, yeah. Good luck." he says.

I walk over to Drew ask him what the problem is.

"Dude, the bartender just told me he saw Greg pour some of our drinks into his."

Not surprised.

"Ah, shit. Really?" I say. Putting on my best surprised reaction.

"Yeah," Drew reacts, "He was supposed to be fuckin' sober dude."

It is a shame to see this happen to be honest. I could be to blame. I just stink of excess and addiction. A smell too familiar to an alcoholic. It makes me sick honestly. The smell of an addict. Well, I suppose I make myself sick than.

"Well, what are we going to do?" I ask.

"I don't know dude, but I am not bringing that fuckin' guy home!"

"Damn man, that is pretty cold." I say. I can't completely comment however, as I don't know the full story. I bet it's a good one though.

"Cold? Dude, do you realize this kid once got drunk and sent a message to my ex asking her to send him a picture of her vagina?" He asks.

"No shit?" I say. I knew it was good.

"Yeah bro! He said to her, 'Send me a beave' shot so I can pop my load.' Such a fucking weirdo."

"Send me a *beave*' shot so I can *pop* my load?" I say. I simply needed to clarify.

That has got to be one of the most perfectly terrible things you can say to someone. A 'beave' shot. Like a Beaver. Who the hell calls a vagina a beaver anymore? But "pop my load." Has to be the greatest metaphor for ejaculating I have ever heard. I was starting to like this guy. Secretly, of course.

"Yeah dude, fucked up isn't it?" Drew asks.

"Oh yeah, totally dude." I say, quite sarcastically.

A brief pause in the conversation happened which built considerable suspense. I decided to ask the question everyone wanted to know.

"Well, like… So, did she send the picture though?"

Drew snapped back to reality and looks at me like he wanted to kill me and says:

"What the fuck is wrong with you Brucie? Why the hell would you ask me that? Do you know how hurt she was?"

"Look, I am sorry Drew. I really am. But buddy, you're *kinda*' being a bitch."

He did not like that.

Drew made a fist that I quickly noticed and try to grab to calm him down. He got very close to my face and began shouting about "his ex" this, and "Greg" that. At this point, I was starting to feel a bit of nihilism overflow me. I had to stop him.

I let go of my hand and slowly put my finger in front of his mouth and made the "shh.." noise to accompany the action. He was steaming mad. But he seized to yell. At this point the whole bar was looking at us and I could see

Greg in the background guzzling my drink down his throat. No matter, best he is drunk for this.

"Look Drew, buddy, I love ya' alright? But, you seriously are being a bit soft here. Look, I mean who care if the guy drinks. It is his life. If he wanted to take a drink today, we couldn't do anything to stop it. He was either full of shit when we picked him up or he played us after the fact. The important thing to remember, Drew, is that we are here for him."

Listen to me, I almost sound like a good person here.

Drew was more than ready to respond by the time he did.

"Be here for him? Brucie, the only reason I invited his ass is because I thought he was reforming himself and *now* look at him..."

We look over to find that he is now swooning some helpless older woman to persuade her to buy him a drink. I will admit, it didn't look good.

"So to be quite honest Brucie, I am bailing. He is *your* problem now."

I was shocked at what he said.

"My problem? What do you mean? I don't even know Greg at all. You picked him up from under a bowling alley, how the hell am I supposed to take care of this mess?"

"I don't know." Drew says. "But I trust you'll figure it out."

Drew headed for the door quite quickly. I see it grab the attention of Greg, who now had his face in the wrinkled bosom of this older madam. Shaking his head from left to right, flailing his lips and screaming "motorboat!" every time he comes up for air. She was thrilled, and for him, it was a non stop booze cruise, and I was aboard!

I walk over to Greg, and slap my hand on his back and say:

"What's up you dirty dog? Enjoying those coconuts?"

He stopped his motor boating and began to speak.

"Hell yeah bro, I am a motor boaty-boy!"

I start laughing hysterically and signaled the bartender for another beer. No use in fighting it now. The dude is smashed. I might as well get on his level.

It started out with a few beers. Then, when I went outside to catch a cigarette with some plumbing union worker who was explaining the finer points of porn compilation movies, I had been slipped some of the white powder in an extraordinary fashion via the worker's unique glass vial fed, mechanically actuated powder sniffing apparatus. Upon reentry to the atmosphere several minutes later we returned into the bar where the working class man bought myself and some bimbo at the bar a couple shots of Irish whiskey because he was an enthusiast of such. I noticed that Greg is gone and the old woman he was with is also absent from the bar. This could be beneficial to my cause. Now, when I have to get out of here, I won't have to pay for the poor cab driver to find a decrepit bowling alley to dump the drunk lonely guy at. I heard a bustle of sorts and the worker and his prostitute looking catch for the night start open mouth kissing at the bar. This caught me off guard as her flailing scarf knocked over several drinks that other patrons had bought for her in an attempt to win her affection. They must have been kissing for no longer than two whole minutes before an angry woman ripped through the front door wearing athletic clothes and a pair of running shoes, clearly not bar attire. She ran up behind this worker, pulled her shoe off and cocked back her arm and wacked the man's head with her shoe. Subsequently hitting the top of the head of the bimbo with it at the same moment.

"You fuckin' piece of shit cheating mother-"

She cocks back again, and again, and keeps blasting the man in the face with the shoe.

I guess it must have been his wife. Funny, he never mentioned he was married. I decided to take a step back as to not get hit in the cross fire. The sound that shoe was making when it cracked on his skull was something to behold, but I wanted nothing to do with it. The man puts his hands up to block the shots to which she just grabbed a hold of his wrist and kept ripping at him with the shoe. It was vicious to watch.

As he tried to stand up, he kept slipping on the rainy muddy mess that coated the bar floor. Hitting the chairs with his other hand to try to block the shots, and also keep his balance while drunk and on the slick floor. He finally gets a hold of the shoe and pushes the woman back while at the same time losing his footing and sliding heavily on the floor. He lost his balance and hit the deck like a ton of bricks. Bashing his face, and knocking himself out. The wife wasn't done though. She just immediately focused on the bimbo, and quite majestically, spear tackled the make up covered, promiscuous harlot. The shoe came down like lightning. Just popping and crashing as the sole of the rubber sneaker contacted the fleshy parts of her face.

I am in total disbelief of what the hell I am witnessing. The bartender was freaking out, trying to pull this woman off of the other, it seemed like he didn't have it handled as he was trying not to get any of the muck from the floor on his clothes.

I see Greg exit the back hall with a much more disheveled looking older woman with him. They part ways and he doesn't even notice the all out brawl happening on this awful sludge covered floor. Nor the seemingly dead man just laying there unconscious. He just walks over to me and says:

"I need a drinky."

He reached over and grabbed three of the half-empty fruity looking drinks that were positioned on the bar in front of where the bimbo was sitting, and pours them all into some random empty beer glass that was sitting on the bar. Stealing the tip money that was underneath it.

I am silently in awe of this man.

"Dude!" He says.

"Yeah?" I answer.

"You ever have your butt hole licked by a grandma?"

I couldn't help but laugh out loud before responding honestly:
"No Greg, no I have not."

"Oh?! You have *got* to try it!" Greg exclaimed.

"Pretty good, huh?" I ask, in support.

"Dude, it's like everything you love about Christmas, but with a bit of a twist. That twist being, an old lady French kisses your bottom."

"Greg, oh god, please stop. What the hell." I say.

He just laughs slightly maniacally and went about drinking his super cocktail.

"So let me ask you something." I say to Greg.

"Yeah, what's up?"

"So is it true you asked Drew's ex girlfriend to send you a picture of her vagina?"

"Oh, yeah, I did. Drew told you that huh? Yeah, I have a problem with substance abuse and it's been a real-"

I cut him off.

"Yeah yeah yeah, substance abuse sucks, so did you get it?" I ask.

Drew laughs.

"No, she didn't. But I'll tell you what she *did* do. she *did* make out with some random dude at Oktoberfest and spend the weekend in his camper doing lines and hooking up with his friends while Drew was working 60 hours a week at the machine shop in Westchester."

"You're serious?" I say in disbelief.

"Yup. I will tell you this too. Ever since that happened, Drew has blamed me for what she did."

I guess that makes sense now. I could not understand why Drew could invite this guy to do something, but then snap on him just like that when he saw that Greg was drinking. It became clear to me that Greg must have at one point apologized and blamed his actions on the alcohol. But why? What kind of person am I dealing with here?

At this point the fight was wrapping up and the man regained consciousness and took a seat at the bar. His wife hauled over to him and screamed in his face once more while he was trying to just get his bearings straight. He wasn't even on this planet yet and she was yelling at the top of her lungs in his face about the kids, and the house, and the dog. It was a train wreck. Eventually the bartender had to kick her out or else he was calling the cops. I would have called them by now personally. Attempted murder with a damn shoe.

"So why do you still hang out with Drew than if it has been like this?" I ask.

"Well dude, keep in mind, I never meant to screw with Drew, or his girlfriend. She was a bit loose and gave me her phone number one night, well before I knew she was dating Drew. I didn't even find out until Drew shows up to my place and starts yelling at me about how his girlfriend disappeared for a few days and when he checked her phone after she got back he saw a message from me asking for a picture." He answers.

"So Drew thought that *you* were responsible when she was *really* out there just being an idiot with some random dude?"

"Pretty much!" He responds. "She came back and played some sympathy card to him and tried to say I was hitting on her so Drew would be distracted from the situation that she was hiding from him. So when he learned what actually happened, we were cool. To a point. He was still mad about the message, to which I said I was a drunk. We both agreed I shouldn't drink anymore if we are gonna' be friends. Fast forward, and here we are."

"Damn, wow. That is pretty heavy stuff." I say.

I couldn't help but think I screwed that up. Greg was starting to get very visibly drunk. Maybe even a little bit more so than he was letting on. He had stopped talking about the situation and was now yelling at the television about the hockey game being played. He kept saying things to me that I couldn't quite make out clearly as he was slurring his words now. He only had one drink, but it was a pretty heavy one. I catch a glimpse of the bartender looking over at him. A look of misunderstanding came over the bartenders face as he comes to grips what was happening.

I posture up to see what he is looking at. Greg is essentially yelling at the TV screen with this mush look on his face like he is having a stroke or something. All you can comprehend are these breathy guttural noises that he is managing to get out. What the hell is this dude on? I feel like I have been asking that a lot lately.

Maybe he took some drugs with that elderly chick? I don't know how likely that is. She looks too old to be into anything this heavy. He just keeps yelling louder, I think he is really fighting it now. The people still at the bar are looking concerned and the bartender walks over and asks me to:
"Get my friend in line, *please*!"

I agree to try at least, and begin attempting to intervene on Greg.

"Greg! *Greg?* GREG!"

I grab his shirt and pull him down to the bar stool. Noticing he has a pack of cigarettes in his pocket that looks new. He sits down. I can feel how messed up he was. He is hot to the touch, and sweating profusely.

"Greg? You okay buddy?" I ask.

"Yeah man, Brucie! What's up man?" He responds.

Greg's eyes are essentially closed and he is drooling now. My goodness he is not doing great. I have to do something about this.

"Greg? Can you hear me? What did you take? Where did you buy the cigarettes?"

I was trying to see where he got these cigarettes from because maybe they were drugged in some way. This didn't make any sense.

"Uh- meh... I bought those." Greg says.

What the hell? A pack of smokes is about $16 how the hell did he afford that?

Greg let out this snorting noise and let out a long winded:

"Why? You want one?"

It was looking like he was getting more conscious from whatever he was on.

"Yeah, please. Let's go have one." I say.

He agrees and opens the pack and grabs two cigarettes and puts one in his mouth and hands me one. As soon as it touched his lips it looked like whatever he was on hit him again. He slouched in his seat with the cigarette in his mouth. He was out cold. Just like that. I snapped my fingers near him a couple times. Nothing.
"Damn it."

I tie up my shoes and head outside to try and calm down the emotion I was feeling now. Now I have to deal with this shit. It could be worse by far. But I just don't want to be a babysitter to this guy right now. I have no idea what this guy is on. Is it these cigarettes? I bring the cigarette up to my nose and smell it to see if it has any type of strange smell to it. Nothing. It smells like the average chemicals of a cigarette. This means nothing though as maybe it is some new space age stuff designed to mess people up. That's a chance I am willing to take.

I spark the cigarette and take a few puffs. Tastes normal and fine. I am looking periodically through the window of the bar at Greg passed out, now face first on the bar. This wasn't good. But in my mind, I couldn't seem to understand the gravity of what was actually taking place beyond my vision at the other end of the bar. I finished the smoke and went back inside to check on Greg. He was still out. I try again to wake him up. Flicking and pinching. He didn't react at all.

He is breathing really slow. I can tell he was out cold. Well, what the hell am I supposed to do. I didn't even notice that people on the other side of the bar are gawking at us. Speculating how terrible it was that some junkie overdosed in their bar. He wasn't a junkie though, as far as I know, and he didn't overdose as far as I know. For some reason at that moment I decided I want another cigarette. Maybe it was my subconscious wanting a reason to escape the situation by going outside which was serene in a way.

I reach into Greg's pocket, grab his pack of cigarettes and take two from the pack. I put one behind my ear as I heard the people on the other end of the bar start commenting on what I was doing. What *was* I doing? Stealing cigarettes from an unconscious man. Damn Brucie, what the hell. This is when I heard some people say something to the bartender:

"Look at these fuckin' heroin addicts over here man!"

I could see an older patron say this to the bartender. The bartender silently responding to the group beyond my ears reach.

"Look, he is stealing fuckin' cigarettes from the dead one!"

You hopefully never have to feel this type of shame in your life. I could hear them roasting me a bit more as I sheltered my emotion to try not to freak out.

I snapped when I heard one say:

"The world is going to shit!"

I couldn't keep quiet any longer.
"Ah!! You know what!? You fuckin' lush's don't know anything! I used to be one of you! You all think you are all so great. From your bar stool, through your glass, you are judging me! You mean nothing! You are all slaves in an uncertain world and you live your life by the rules like the little bitches you truly are!"

I realize in a short moment that Greg was likely drugged. The idiot took a bunch of secondhand drinks that were laying on the bar and mixed them all into one. Someone probably dropped some sort of pill in one of them to try and take advantage of her. Unfortunately, it makes no difference now. I am already erupting.

"So, if you all could please! Stop judging what the hell you are seeing and call a damn ambulance for my friend, I think he has been drugged or something!" I conclude.

The bartender responds with:

"We already did, scumbag."

"Fuck you!" I say.

I turn around and leave the bar, only to see the ambulance run towards the bar, and I stopped them.

"Hey! You guys are going into that bar right?"

"Yes, sir." The medics respond.

"Okay cool. Look, I think the dude blacked out in there, was drugged or something. He kept taking drinks off the bar that were left there. I may be wrong but it makes sense to me." I say. Hoping maybe it would help the two resuscitate Greg.

"Okay, great. Thanks a lot sir." They say, before continuing with their task.

I walk down the street. It was such a gross night. I pulled one of the cigarettes out of my pocket and light it with the matches that I took from inside the pack Greg had. It only stays lit for a short second before a falling rain drop lands on the edge of the cigarette, extinguishing the ember, and breaking my morale.

"Mother-"

I was less than amused. I wanted to get out of there, quickly. I see a police car with its lights and sirens blaring, burning through the corner of the block I was walking on. Time to play it cool. It pulled up sharply and diagonally to the bar. The cop exit's the car in a hurry, with a small medic bag in his clutch. Damn, I hope Greg was going to be okay. Who the hell knows how much drugs he had in his system, and of what type.
Something about the thought of drugs made me think of Larry.

"Oh shit! Larry!"

I had forgot that Larry was last known to be stuck in the floor of the house we are living at. Man, I am really messing up these days. I decided to catch the next train back home. The night was finished. My buzz was wearing off and I was beginning to feel a bit of a detox trauma coming. I walked about 13 blocks to the nearest subway platform. I was lucky enough to be able to afford to use these transit systems. It was nothing to the normal people. But to a worthless imbecile like me, this was bitter sweet. At one point, I would laugh at people using public transit. But now, I somewhat envy them. It is all a matter of perspective.

After a few stops on the subway, I arrived at the central terminal for the Eastbound trains. I paid cash for the ticket at the kiosk, waited around a bit, and boarded my train.

I was accompanied by several teenagers and young adults who earlier, had headed into the city to go to a fabled bar that caters to the underage. All of which I deciphered from over hearing their loud, drunk conversation. All of them had over indulged and were fading in their seats. One was unlucky enough to get a touch of the spins on the train and got sick. Spewing whatever they were drinking all over the floor. It smelled like black licorice.

I hate that stuff. It reminds me of a time when I drank way to much and threw up the same vile substance onto an off white plush sofa I had in my apartment at the time. Then being so hung over for two days that I didn't clean it up. I didn't own a truck so instead of bringing it to a dumpster or something I just lugged the whole sofa out to the front curb and left it there. The mess sat in the sun for five whole days, plaguing its awful stench on anyone who was unlucky enough to walk by it. How embarrassing.

I decided to get up and change my seat to be more alone. Figuring this was as good a time as any to get some shut eye. So I did.

* * * * * * * * * * * * * * * * * * *

I am abruptly awakened about forty minutes later by a woman's bag hitting the seat next to me. She is getting on the train to depart, and is dressed rather well to be boarding a train in this part of town. Especially this late at night. I ask her:

"Sorry to bother you, but what stop is this?"

"It's no problem. This is West Harbor." She responds.

"Okay, great. Thank you."
West Harbor was two towns over from mine. I likely had only a few minutes left on this train so I shook it off and try to wake myself up. I still had a bit of a walk to get from the train station to the house.

"Where are ya' headed?" She asks me.

"Oh, uh. Smog Town."

"Oh…" She scoffs.

She clutches her purse and tries not to keep the conversation going. As many have figured out, Smog Town isn't the best place to be. I was used to this by now, I am actually surprised she even answered my question let alone asked me where I was going. I mean I must look like a wet stinky dog. Maybe she is into wet stinky dogs. You never know. That's what is strange about all this. I could be clean cut and smelling like $500 cologne and if I said I live in Smog Town, she likely would have looked at me even worse. Asking, what is this guy is doing on this train, in this part of town. But wait, she is dressed pretty well, and she smells nice too. What the hell was she doing in this part of town, at this time. Well I am not going to start with chivalry now.

"Scuse' me. Can I ask you something?" I ask her.
She was taken back by this advance. Obviously scared for her life.

"Uh.. *Sure*? What's going on?" She responds

"Well, I see that you are obviously quite fancy. You know like the ketchup? See I was just wondering well, what the fuck are you doing here?"

She was obviously shocked by this question.

"Excuse me? What the fuck did you just say to me motherfucker?"

Oh, see now I see why she was out this late.

"Look, I didn't mean to offend you. You just seem, fancy. Like- like-"

She interrupts me.

"Like ketchup. Yeah, I got that."

A pause in the conversation.

"Well? What's the answer?" I ask.

"I'm a dancer. Duh!" She snaps.

Damn, I'm an idiot. She was dressed quite well for a stripper though.

"Oh, see, that makes sense."

The alarm sounds on the subway letting the occupants know that Smog Town was the next stop.

"This your stop? *Scumbag.*" She says.

I stand up and snap back.

"I am not a scumbag!"

I exit the train. The lady clutching her bag pensively with shock in her eyes.

Smog town is humid and dark. Sunrise would be coming soon. The signal that the bars would be closing and all the poor saps and one night stands would be ready to stumble to their respected homes, be it most likely a nice drunk drive to one of each others homes for a quick shag and cigarette. It was also the time of night that the low lives like myself are stumbling home from a rough night out, or just looking for a place to crash in the sun so they can dry out from the rain and damp that the night had brought. This time of day was a high risk time. The regulars are all either waking from a slumber or beginning their modest day or getting their kids ready for school. It is a somber time for me. A time when I would often find myself in awe of my surroundings. Questioning how it is that I became to model what I am now. A dirty, wet, stinky lackluster drug user. A "once upon a time" type. Always questioning if my time had come and pass, much like the beauty of the passing sunrise. With that sunrise would often bring a sober moment. A moment of clarity to all the nonsense that I had gotten myself into the night or day before. How pathetic. Stop feeling bad for yourself.

The minuscule rain drops created an interesting backdrop against the warm yellow of the streetlights. A hue that the rising sun was in a race to match. I was in a race for the creature comforts that I had recently acquired. The warm house. Look at me, acting like it was mine. I better get to walking.

I started heading east, shortly reaching the entrance to the park that Drew and I had been a little earlier. I wonder if Christina was near by. I start to walk faster as it dawned to me that Larry was still potentially stuck in a hole in the ceiling at home. I am impressed by my own speed, but as I was walking I smell something pretty awful. Enough that it made me stop and question my route.

"Oh damn. What the hell is that stench?" I say to myself.

I was interrupted by the crash and alarm of homeless Christina, Larry's 'ex girlfriend.'

She fell out from behind an alleyway between two brick houses with her ass exposed as she tripped over her underwear and pants around her ankles. Taking out a trash can on her way down.

"What the hell!?" I exclaim.

"HEY! Quit looking *pervert*! RAPE! RAAPE!" She screams as she laid on the ground pulling up her pants and getting herself together.

"SHH!! *Shut up!*" I say, jumping back as I could see the interior lights of a neighboring house turning on in response to her cries. She stopped floundering around on the wet ground and caught a glimpse of my face.

She stops yelling.

"Oh. It's *you*." She says.

"Christina, What the fuck!? That isn't cool, You could get me killed!" I say.

"Oh, nobody cares man-" She picks herself up off the ground.
"I got raped a week ago, just right over there. Nobody gave a shit." She continues.

"Oh my god, Christina, that's terrible." I say.

"Yeah, there is a better chance of someone joining in than killing *you*." She says.
"So what are you doing?"

"Nothing, I am heading home, well, to your Grandma's place. Speaking of which. Did you talk to your Mother?" I ask.

"Yeah, that bitch already hates me. Hey, you're heading up there?!" She asks, totally disregarding my question.

"Yeah?" I say, curious as to why she would ask again.

"Cool, I am gonna' come with you than." She says.

"What? No you're not!" I exclaim.

"Uh, Yes I am! She is *my* Grandmother after all motherfucker!"

I thought about it for a second, and how bad this girl smelled. She could likely use a break and I am in the mood that I can sympathize with her struggle, even if the choices were her own. But I don't know if they were anyway. Who is to say she wasn't abused, or introduced to drugs very early.

"Sure, okay yeah I guess you're right. But you gotta' take a damn shower when we get there."

"Yeah whatever man, cool." She says.

"So what the hell were you doing back there anyway?" I ask.

"I was taking a shit and I thought you were the cops you narc." She responds.

I laugh a bit but am also a bit disgusted.

"Well, alright."

Christina and I started walking south after we reached the end of that block. In the direction of the home. The sun was beginning to rise and it was a welcome bit of sensory relief from the scent that Christina's sweat pores was putting out. It was almost unreal. The wet humid air was hitting her like rainwater hits an old greasy dog.

You can see some weird stuff early in the morning. People, rushing to get places breeds mistakes not normally seen by the likes of noon sunshine. The casual sideswiped car, the 'near miss' hit and run, the coffee spill walk of shame, and my favorite, the dysfunctional family.

A family wakes to begin the day. The mother pops a pill, starts the coffee machine and begins making lunch for her kids. The father rises, takes a shit, hops in the shower and begins washing as the son heads into the bathroom to pee. His toilet flush scorches the father. He screeches at the boy. As he has done this several times before. Then the daughter arrives in the downstairs bathroom to ready herself. She starts the shower. Totally ignorant of 'hot water heaters' and 'tank reservoirs,' she lets the shower run as she squats on the toilet to do her business. She waits for the water to warm to her liking, which will only happen after the father has lost his patience with the ordeal and just cuts his scorching, then cold shower short. She then flushes the toilet and the water shoots out steaming hot. So she waits. As this is happening the son is in his room playing with every thing he can as long as it means that he is not readying himself for school. Meanwhile, his mother, who has just finished making three lunches, will walk in on him 10 minutes before the bus is to arrive, and the boy is only wearing his underwear and a t-shirt that he slept in. By the time this family is ready to leave the house. The mother is already spiking her coffee with whiskey and the father is wishing he just wore a damn condom. This is all evident by the haste and attitude visible by the family as they exit their townhouse and head to their respected destinations. No hugs goodbye. Just hot engines and cold shoulders. I think I was a little jealous to be honest.

Finally we arrive to the house. Christina looks like she was about to pass out, but she might have been going through some come down from the drugs.

"Hey, we are here Christina, are you okay?" I ask.

Yeah, just a little… Sick." She replies.

"What? Dope?" I ask.

"Yeah." She nods.

"Well do you want to get some? Like are you going to be okay?" I ask.

"Yeah I want to fucking get some! But no… I don't want it, and yes. I will be okay. I really just want to get clean." She says.

My eyes could have popped right out of my skull.

"Huh? Well alright man. Let's get you clean." I say as I grab her by her wrist and guide her towards the front door of the house.

"Christina look, you gotta' go in there, clean yourself up really well, and just pick a room. Okay? You can get clean here, you have a chance, and think how proud your family will be." I say.

She agrees in a shrug as we opened the door and she scurried away to a bathroom to vomit.

"Well, that was weird." I say to myself, noticing that the front door was unlocked.

Though I was slightly relieved that she was away from me for a moment and her stench was in the bathroom with her. That girl had a hell of a road ahead of her. Coming off drugs can be a nightmare to say the least.

"Larry!? Larrryyy!?" I yell as I walk around the place. I heard nothing. I began to fear the worst. Is it possible that one day stuck in a ceiling is enough to kill a man?

I run up the stairs of the house and sprint towards the bathroom that contained the stairs to the attic, sprinting up those stairs as well. Only to find that when I observed the massive hole in the floor where Larry broke through, he was gone.

"What the, hell?" I say, as I approach the hole. Slowly and with caution. Not knowing if this floor I was walking on would abruptly give way under my weight and trap me between a wall like Larry. I look down the hole that was left. A strange weak spot in the home. Just a piece of weak floor board that covered a closet sized empty space left over after framing the upstairs bedrooms some 100 or so years ago.

Not a bad place to hide something potentially.

"No Larry here."

He wasn't in the hole. So he musthave figured a ways out, and with what looks like without much effort. I turned around and headed back down the attic stairs into the bathroom that they lead to. I reached the landing of the stairs and closed the outward opening door to expose the hallway that would lead me downstairs. However, upon closing the door, a large male figure appeared and grabbed me by my shirt.

"What the fuck are *you* doing here!?" He yelled as he threw me by my dirty T-shirt down the hallway.

I feel he must have tossed me three or four yards easily. This man is huge. A brute of an old westerner, shaved head, stocky build. Stood easily at six and a half feet tall. There is no way I am defending myself against this guy, especially at the moment. Half dead and recovering from a pharmaceutical beating.

He began to approach me.

"Whoa whoa WHOA! Buddy *LISTEN-*" I plea as he grabs me by the neck and belt strap and threw me down the stairs.

That fucking hurt. Those stairs are quite steep, however, he was kind enough to not throw me too far down them. Much of the impact was me sliding and rolling down the other wise steep and wooden stairs.

"Ooh, fuck! Ow… Damn," Is all I could get out as I roll around on the ground in agony.

A figure caught my eye in the kitchen as I crawled around on the landing. It was the women from before. Christina's mother, Carmen.

"Heh… He- Hey! CARMEN!" I say to her.

"Holy shit! It's you?" She responds.

By that time, The big bastard was on the last step of the stairs and was ready to give me another round of beating. Luckily, Carmen called him off.

"Bruce! Stop!" She says. He reacts like a dog to her.
I let out a marvelous sigh of relief.

"I know him, he is fine!" She says to him.

"Huh? Oh, sorry mate." He says, in a slightly British tone. He then grabs me by the wrist and pulls me to my feet. My bones popping and cracking from the travel down the stairs.

"Oh shit!" I say as I feel the pain set in. "It's alright there, Bruce. I like your name by the way." I add.

"What the hell is that supposed to mean!?" He snaps at me. Changing my attitude from friendly to terrified.

"Oh I am just taking a piss mate, cheers!" As he slaps my back, damn near sending me flying.

I hobble over to the kitchen, and sit down on one of the chairs that populate the dining room table. Carmen just looks at me as I sit down in silence. Not focused too much on talking, more so on keeping my shit together, I think my collar bone is broken.

"Look, before Bruce here clips her with some knuckledusters, I figure I should tell you. Christina is in the bathroom."

"Christina is here?!" She snaps, "Christina!" She howls as she calls her name and runs towards the bathroom.

Bruce is looking at me like he wants to help but also wants to punch my face in. I am still not sure why. Carmen reaches the bathroom door and starts knocking on it and saying Christina's name in a soft and loving voice.
"Christina? Honey? You in there?" She asks.

There was a bit of silence.

"Christina?" She asks. She starts to wiggle the locked door knob and knock on the door a little more frantically.

"Christina, please open the door! Please?! It is okay! We are here for you!" She says. But still no answer. I began to start to fear the worst as I heard Carmen start to hit the door more frantically and her tone shift to a more interrogating sound.

"Christina, please! You have *options*!"

Oh boy how I love hearing that. "You have options!" Such a dependable old saying. When someone has shit luck, "hey, you have options!" Someone facing hell,"hey, you have options." I think a lot of mankind's struggles have boiled down to too many damn options. People will spend their whole lives living by the advice of their parents, or teachers, and then face an existential crisis in their later years because they didn't live *their* life. While on the other hand, individuals who had little to no guidance as a child often struggle tremendously in the fact that they just want someone to tell them what to do. So they can rest easy in making the right choice for once. The caveat to all this being that nobody really has any options at all. You create the circumstance that arises from the circumstance that you created prior. Much like every action is the genesis action to the next.

"Don't move!" Bruce says as he runs over to the bathroom to assist Carmen.

I hear him approach the door and knock twice before saying:

"Christina, love. Open it or it comes down!"
A stern warning that proceeded him twisting the lock winder so hard it snapped the armature and he pushed open the door.

The house fell silent.
"Christina? Honey? What are you doing?" Carmen says in slight relief.

Good, she wasn't in there dead or something. That would have been a real bummer. I decided to get up and walk over to the hallway that lead to the bathroom. I could hear Christina as she says:

"Nothing mom, just feeling a little sick is all."

"Sick? Why? What are you on? Did he give you something?" Carmen says to Christina. I could immediately feel the tension rise.

"No! Nothing like that. I am getting clean mom. I am done with it. I... I am gonna' *keep* it." Christina says.

"I am going to *get* my shit together, and I am going to *keep* the baby."

I think we all just entered zero gravity when that news hit the room. I hadn't felt so special in a long time. To bear witness to such a moment like that was moving. I see a tear fall from Carmen's eye and fall onto the arm of Christina. A smile on Carmen's face as she rubbed her daughters back and welcomed this news.

I felt my own nose begin to burn as I witnessed the innocence of a street rat become reborn. I was about to tear up myself. Maybe there is hope for us. Maybe we will be alright after all. Bruce let out a deep exhale and put his hands on his hips. He looks over at me. A bit of a twinkle in his eye, as if he might have been just as moved as I am.

"Well fuck, I ain't much of a sucker for this warm stuff mate." He says, as he approaches me at the end of the hallway.

"How 'bout a beer, huh?" He asks.

"Sure, sounds great." I say as I walk with him towards the kitchen.

One of the rules of being a man is, whenever there is a strong feminine loving moment, there is absolutely *no* shame in just falling back and letting them be. Too many a father have forgotten this rule, and their daughters resent them for it. Sometimes their wives as well. Just as one of the responsibilities of a Women would be to care and nurture, the responsibility of man is to remain strong, deep rooted, and a foundation for your loved ones to grow on.

Bruce opened the refrigerator and grabbed two beers from a 12 pack that looks fresh. A day drinker I see. We will get along well. He cracks open both bottles with one hand, something I had never seen done before, and hands me one. We take a sip. A good German Pilsner. Taste almost like a burnt piece of bread.

"So, what's your deal mate?" He asks me.

"Oh me? Well, my name is Brucie." I extend my arm to shake his hand and my shoulder and elbow pop and crack from the beating I just got.

"Ah, shit. I'm sorry bruv. I guess that 'like your name' comment makes sense now, dunnit?"

He shakes my hand and smiles, but must not have realized his catchers mitt of a hand was crushing mine, and I was about at my pain threshold. I pull my hand away in nervous desperation. Switching the cold beer over to that one shortly after to try and numb the pain with the cold glass of the bottle. There was a bit of a silence.

"So what's your deal Bruce? Are you Christina's father?" I ask him.

"Actually mate, I'm not. Carmen and I started seeing each other shortly after Christina decided she wanted to be a street rat. Carmen started going to an anger management class and we met there. Her and I had gone out a few time before so I was a little familiar with the situation with her."

"No shit? Jeez you got a hell of a heart to take on all this." I say.

He laughs.

"Well son it wasn't really my intention. Carmen is a sweetheart and all, and she is quite the looker. But I didn't know how much of a handful that her daughter was. To be honest, I love Carmen so much at this point, I wish I could just get rid of Christina if it would just let Carmen relax for a minute. She may look calm and cool on the outside, but the Woman is stressed. Rightfully so, I suppose." He takes a swig from the bottle.

I nod my head in agreement.
"Yeah, I can feel that."

"So what, are you the father or something, mate?" He asks.

"Oh, *No*. N-n-n no! *Certainly* not, But I think I *might* know who is." I say, as Larry comes to my mind.

"Oh yeah? Is that right? Care to share mate?" He says, looking rather pensive and quietly very interested.

I really didn't want to piss this dude off again. Not with the bottle in his hand. Not with the knowledge of his day drinking, and long history of anger issues. Not with my wad of cash and drugs hidden in the backyard. That is my nest egg. If I can just get to that I will be alright.

"Uh, well man. I mean, she hooked up with my friend Larry. But that was like a day or two ago, and I think that it was only some mouth stuff anyway." I say, preparing to have my face punched in.

"Get the fuck out of here mate, Larry? The chubby bloke we pulled out of the upstairs ceiling a little while ago?"

I was visibly relieved.
"Yes! Exactly! The one and only!"

"Nah, no offense. But I don't think so mate. Christina sleeps around son. It could be quite literally any one of the low lives in this town. Or none at all for all we are concerned. Not like we are going to go after him right?"

"Very true." I respond. "So hey, where is Larry now?"

"Oh, we called an ambulance for the chap. He cut his sides all up in the attempt to get him out. They took him to Metro Hospital." Bruce says.

Well I suppose that wasn't the worst thing. As long as he keeps his mouth shut, which he usually is good for. Matter of fact, I can recall a time where Larry got caught stealing a 12 oz beer from the beverage once, and when the cop asked where he was going, Larry answered honestly with 'I am on my way back to the Elementary school to fuck around in the dumpster.' The police officer just shrugged him off as an idiot and let him go. On second thought, maybe that cop was just a front.

"Shit, so Larry is in the hospital, eh? Well that bites."

At this point Carmen and Christina both hailed from the bathroom hallway. Carmen propping Christina by her shoulders, Nursing her up to her bedroom to try and shake the detox. I could see her coming down hard. I hope she survives. Sometimes a personal habit isn't what kills them, it's quitting the habit that triggers the white light. I glimpse at Christina as she passes me by, a nervous gracious smile donned her face. It somewhat warmed my heart. Almost enough to make *me* want to quit. But who the hell am I kidding. That Microwave full of narcotics was screaming my name and I was hearing it loud and clear.

On that note.

"Hey Bruce, listen. I know this may not be the time, but I was renting here. Is that still happening do you know?" I ask.

"Yeah, afraid not mate. Carmen and I are going to spend terms here until we can get the estate figured out. We were lucky enough that Larry was stuck in the ceiling or else he could have robbed Carmen's Mother blind. So unfortunately son, your gonna' have to piss off. Sorry mate."

I couldn't really say I was surprised to hear this. I was totally not deserving of such a nice place.

"Oh, well alright. It's no big deal I guess. Can I ask one thing though. Is there like, a backpack, or something I can use to put my clothes in for the mean time? I had a garbage bag with some clothes in it and I don't know. I just don't want to haul it around."

"Yeah, yeah yeah. Actually there is one you can use. Funny you should ask. Carmen and I pulled some garbage from the attic and left it out on the side of the house. There were one or two bags out there you could use." Bruce says quite wittingly.

"Perfect."
I finished the last of the Brew, which had restored a little bit of life to me. Something I desperately needed in this time. As I was about to head basically back to where I just came from to find Larry.

"Well, Bruce, It's been a pleasure sir." I say.

"Ah, Brucie. The pleasure is all mine." Bruce responds.

"Cheers." He added as he sipped his beer with one hand, and a two finger salute with the other.

I make my way for the door and looped up the side of the house where the trash is kept. There is a pile of old rubbish. From old magazines, to wooden nick-knacks, and all the shit you would find in a Grandmother's attic. I start to dig though it, only finding two things that could be suited as a "bag."

One, was a leather bound suitcase that was warped so bad it wouldn't close properly anymore. The other, a pink Cabbage Patch Kids backpack that had honestly seen better days. It had this awfully creepy face on it that featured long bright yellow yarn protruding from the face fabricated into the bag. It was dusty and knotted. The face, missing an eye and covered in brown dirt from being wherever it was tucked away at for the last couple decades. Slim pickings.

I walk back to the shed where the microwave is. Rummaged a bit, and transferred the contents over to my bright pink backpack. Well at least I am not carrying around a microwave anymore. But I definitely still feel a bit exposed. One wrong move and I am facing a long, long deal of legal problems. Cops would love to bust a homeless man with a pocket full of stolen blood money and a children's backpack full of narcotics.

Back to town I go. The feeling in my mind was a lot like the uncomfortable feeling that a peak of the sun will bring on a rainy day. A feeling of content for the darkness, and fear of the light. It made no difference, I have to go.

Larry was at a hospital. The last damn place I want to go right now, even though my body *feels* broken. Unpleasant thoughts of times once past. Losing loved ones. Pain and suffering. Too much of all the things that a chronic drug user would often use drugs simply to escape. Hell, the last time I was in a hospital I was leaning over the body of my adoptive father.

I remember telling his doctor "that eight years of medical school means nothing if you can't do a fucking thing!"

They were less than pleased as I was forcibly removed, and barred from seeing the last moments of my father. I think he would have been saying the same though. Again, it makes no difference. Such a disgusting filthy world we inhabit. All the poor animals and fauna that are cursed to be here while we are. No wonder I was so down, it was all doom and gloom. I guess I need to take another train back to the damn metro area and get Larry from that hell hole. So be it.

My mind has taken my feet rather far without much notice. Which is okay, I am so tired at this point I did not want to be doing any of this. I walked by the basement dwelling that Larry and I used to live in. The owners had the door open, and are moving out all the trash and useless shit that Larry and I had brought there throughout the time we lived there. The owners wife was raveling up the stolen extension cord that powered our life. Simple times. Much more simple than now. For some reason It brought up the circumstance that lead me to even be in that shit hole.

"What the fuck are you doing, Brucie?" I ask myself.

By this time I got too main street, downtown was rather empty. I decide to take a different route to the train station, and walked past a store front that had particular meaning to me. I previously knew the owner of this store. An old black man who ran a particularly special business and could find things that were often very rare. Not like drugs or people or anything like that, but if you wanted some ancient relic, or collectors item, he could find it. I could almost feel the hallucination, as I see a younger version of my self pull up to the curb in that hot convertible that I once owned. A slick haired, clean and warm young man. I swore I could even feel the sun on my shoulders. Instead, it was the heat of the hand from a man cupping my shoulder, snapping me back to the cold world that was actually around me.

"Brucie!" He says.
I look over in this direction, but really did not want to leave the world I was witnessing.

It was Larry.

"Larry! Dude, what *is* going on?" I say.
They must have cleaned him up in the hospital because his hair isn't all greasy and he didn't smell like a wet dog.

"Nothing!" He says.
He then cocked back his fist and punched me in the gut nearly as hard

as he could.

I let out a "Hhumph!" noise as the wind fled from my stomach. I took that hit bad.

"*THAT'S* FOR LEAVING ME IN THE CEILING YOU FUCK!" Larry screamed at me.

Of course other people on the street took notice at this and justifiably avoided it. With good reason.

"Larry, you fucking asshole!" I wanted to hit him so badly but the chance of getting arrested with all the drugs on me was far too much a risk. He is still yelling at me on the street, but I can't really make out what he is saying. I just got my wits together quickly and headed in the opposite direction. Really it is all I can do at this point. Larry wasn't about to follow me, and with good reason I might add. I left the dude stuck in a hole in the ceiling for who knows how long. But I guess at least I didn't need to go find his ass. He was in town.

I decided I would just go find a hotel that was empty enough to give me a room with no identification and on cash only. If I remember right, there is a gross hourly rate motel not far from here. It isn't great, but there was no way in hell I was sleeping on the street again. Not with the cache of goods. Not with the amount of sleep I was running on.

I decided again to walk. It wasn't that far and I could afford to do so at the moment. Damn though, Larry got me good. I guess I really pissed the guy off. Not the first time. Likely will not be the last either.
I was beginning to get dirty looks on the street from passing strangers. They must have been seeing my disheveled form and truly terrible demure and figured I was better suited for stealing their possessions than saying hello. I could really use a shower and a nap.

It is only about a quarter of a mile to get to the motel. But the dreadful heat and humidity at the moment has me sweating like a cold glass of water. I am positive that my aroma was that of something foul or even dead. I'm fortunate enough to not notice my own stench though. A luxury anyone down wind of me did not afford. Cars pass me by like fleeting feelings of discontent. But I carry in tow my love for the surroundings. Things could always be different. This could be worse. Those punks from the other night could find me walking and beat the ever living shit out of me. The police could put me at the scene of a murder, even if it was justified. I could be robbed, mugged, shot, stabbed, run over. Shit, even busted...
But I'm not.

A few thousand horrible humid steps later and I arrive at the motel. It appeared that there was only one car in the lot. Likely a prostitute and some John making use of an hour or two and some spare cash. This was that type of place.

'The Grand Prix.'

The Grand Prix is a scuzzy little motel hidden behind an old Chinese food place. Not the most admirable. But it will house me for the night and keep me out of harms way. Sometimes a blessing is hidden, we will see.

I make my way towards the office to buy my way in. A Spanish looking guy with neck tattoos and slick back hair is waiting at the counter speaking with the girl that works there. The conversation was civil, but stopped once I slipped in the screen door. I take off the backpack, as I knew this thing was my meal ticket and I actually couldn't afford to lose it right now. The Spanish guy turns around and looks at me. He winced at my pink backpack and laughs a bit.

Best to just be respectful.
"Hey, how are ya. Name's Bruce." I present my hand to shake.

He looks at it, almost with unfamiliarity. But does accept and shakes my hand.

"Luis, mucho gusto..." He shakes my hand and releases."...órale, what's up with your bag holmes."

The woman behind the counter pops up to take a peak at the bag. As soon as she sees it she busts out laughing and says too him:

"Ay, otro joto gringo!"

He looks at her and busts out laughing. I don't know a ton of Spanish but I think she said it looks gay. I really didn't want any trouble. Too damn tired. I just laugh and say:

"Ay, guys, come on, it's all I have, man."

He laughs, smacks my shoulder, and says:

"Hey we're just fucking with you man, besides, we don't hate!"

They both just bust out laughing, Prodding at the cliche. Which admittedly is pretty funny.
I just try to laugh it off the best I can and proceed to ask the young lady at

the counter if a room is available. It was no wonder this dude was in here. Obviously trying to make a move on her, she was gorgeous.

Long dark hair, perfect symmetrical features, this girl was a painting.
"Hey, look, so do you have a room? I gotta' crash-"

She cut me off..
"Yes, sure no problem. You care what level?"

She is asking if I wanted a ground level or balcony room. In a place like this. I'll take the upper level.
"Uh, you have a balcony room?"

"Yup, take 2B. It's twenty a day." She responds.

$20 a day. Damn, this place is nuts.

"Okay, cool, can I pay cash?" I ask.

"Yeah, But there is a $5 fee for cash."

Luckily I have $25 in my pocket from last night and didn't have to open my bag.

"Alright, cool." I pull the money out of my pocket. It was all damp from being in my pocket for so long on this gross day. Can't have shame now.

I hand her the gross wet money and she dons a disgusted face as the dude next to me laughs.

"Ugh' Qué mierda!" She says.

"Sorry, it's just hot out. I can wash it?" I say, laughing a little bit.

"Yuck! No it's fine. It doesn't matter." She says, as she opens the cash drawer and slaps the wet money on top of the other money in the register.
She throws her hand under the table and grabs the room key for 2B. This was an actual key. Not the door card like modern hotels. So be it. She hands me the key.

"Sweet. Thank you. When is checkout." I ask.

"3 P.M."

"Alright, thanks guys, it was nice meeting y'all." I say as I head for the door and push it open.

"Later, holmes." I hear the man say.

As I walk down the alleyway towards the stairs for the upper deck I hear the two occupants in one room having some pretty rough sex. Not entirely caring that there may be people near by to hear the obscene shit they are saying.

"SHIT ON MY FUCKIN' BALLS!" I hear echo through the parking lot at one point.

Whoa. This is serious.
I head for the stairs and walk up them causally, however, in better spirits after hearing that commotion. It was about to be a hot date between me and that mattress. Here it is, 2B. The key didn't exactly love the lock, I have to wiggle it a little bit, and give extra force to get the knob to turn. Once I managed to get the door to budge I was greeted with a musty old cigarette smell and the usual old, shiny blue mattress with some old bulk sale sheets on it. I locked the door and decided to head for the bathroom and see if there was any towels in the shower. Thankfully, there was. I threw a couple of towels over the mattress before fitting the sheet over it and making it look presentable. There was no blanket, but that didn't matter much to me as it was hot enough. I put the pillows in a case and threw it on the bed. Now for the backpack. There isn't a great place to hide it, not immediately anyway. So I put it at my side and hit the bed hard. Not much support there. Who cares. I am sleeping.

****

I awoke to the sound of the maid slamming on the door, saying something in Spanish. The clock next to me says 3:25 PM. I slept for nearly twelve hours straight. It feels incredible. I jumped up from the bed, to swim over to the door, as this room that I was in felt like a warm swimming pool.

"Alright, alright alright!" I yell as I approach the door and open it.
It is the girl from the front counter.

"Hey, asshole, you missed check out! Now do I need to send Luis up here-" She says rather fiercely.

"Whoa!" I cut her off. "No, n-n-no, nothing like that. I just overslept is all. I would have came down and paid you!"

"Well what the fuck, man? You got more cash or what?" She asks.

"Yes! I do let me just grab it and I'll pay you right now!"

I head over to the bag to grab some money for her. I don't think I actually had exact change. I might only have 20, 50, and 100 dollar bills.

I reach into the cache of money I have and pulled out a $50 bill, and walk it over to her.

"Okay, here, I am sorry. Here is 2 days up front. Is that okay?" I ask.

"Yeah, that's fine. Look, don't oversleep again. I don't want to send my brother up here." She says.

"Oh, okay. Again, I'm sorry I didn't mean for that to happen." I add.

"You better not!" She says. As she walks away I catch a glimpse of her long hair waving over her body. Such a glimpse might make a man crazy. I closed the door and say to myself:

"Her brother?"

I guess that means it's possible, maybe I should ask her out. I look in the mirror that was attached to the dresser. A pale, chewed up looking face greeted me. Messed up, dirty hair and a gross beard. Damn, maybe I should get cleaned up.

After another nap...

****

I woke up to my tooth throbbing. I must have been grinding my teeth again. No real surprise, I was having that stress dream again. The room feels like it is broiling. I am definitely dehydrated. Holy shit. I haven't had any water since Christina's step father offered me a beer after he threw me down the damn stairs. I really know better than to drink the water in this motel. I saw a set of small paper cups on the dresser earlier. So I unwrapped the dusty cellophane that wrapped them and headed to the bathroom to use the sink. I turned on the cool water faucet and was greeted by two egg fart smelling burps from the plumbing before a slow, warm stream began to blow from the faucet. I let it run for a second to hopefully get a bit of a fresher taste. What day is it? I must have skipped any detox just by sleeping. I had paid off the motel manager for two days, and she never came back so it must be just the next day. I peek over to the clock outside the bathroom door frame. 7:45 PM, goodness. It might just be the same day. That would be awful. The water flowing from the sink is running cold and steady now. I am satisfied with that and proceed to drink cup after cup of this mixture of chlorine and sulfur tasting water. Absolutely better than nothing. My mouth was so dry that the water hitting the roof of my mouth felt like the long needed rain landing on an arid high desert full of cracks and ripples from its dry, tortured, weathering decay. The long dried remnant of saliva regaining a bit of salinity in its exposure to the water. It made me remember back to when an old co-worker of mine cited me a fact as we were driving to get lunch one day.

His name was George, he was a pretty typical looking guy. But as we were heading back from getting some food, he had a bottle of fancy imported artesian water brought to your local gas station from a million year old Swiss aquifer. He was pounding the bottle and complained that it "tasted like a diaper." I was a little drawn back by what he meant by saying that the water tasted like a diaper. But he went on to explain about how there was such a high mineral content that it tasted like talc. George was a strange dude to say the least. Anyway, I was telling him one day that you shouldn't drink so fast after eating, like I remember my father telling me once. George was quick to disagree. George went on to say:

"I read a thing once that said how scientists did a test and they found that if you can physically chug water for more than 8 seconds, it means that your body is a liter low on water, and you're getting dehydrated."

I laughed in his face as I figured this was total nonsense. But I feel bad about that now. Because I think if I had a receptacle large enough to facilitate me to be able to chug water for more than 8 seconds I think I would absolutely use it to its full potential.

I must have put back fifteen or so little cups of tap water before I even felt slightly compelled to breath. So I put the cup down and let out a rather loud grunting noise as the water hydrated the severely desperate tissues that it rolled over. As I began to get my bearings straight and splash some cold water on my face and neck to cool me down, it sent shivers up my spine. I could see the sunlight that was blaring into the front facing window begin to turn a more gray color. I look around the room to make sure everything is where I left it. It was. That is good news. I walk over to the window. The feel of this carpet under my toes really made me question having bare feet. It is a mixture of crunchy and damp. Bristles that are too long to be fashionable in this decade, and certainly a cheap leftover color in some warehouse from around the time of the construction of this motel. When I reach the window and peak out, it appeared that a very large rain cloud had moved over the evening sun. Shortly after that, a very cold gust of wind came and shook the motel to its core. It's frigid blast came and went and with it, came a cooling mist of a reward. It was finally cooling down. I could begin to smell the rain coming. I open up the door to the motel and walk out on the balcony. The cloud was massive. It is a deep gray with amazing patches of navy blue. I felt a cool rain drop strike my face, and then it began.

The rain dropped like a bucket of water on this dirty floor of a town. It was always nice to see it actually rain here, instead of the pathetic sun showers and short bouts we usually get. The heavy drops would cut holes in the brown coating of dust and grime, and then slowly work its ways to the lowest parts. Where it would form a temporary river of brown muddy water and grime. This was a relief to say the least, as it was the evening too, so the sun won't just come and make the area an awful humid mess. A nice detoxification.

Rainy nights really are a trophy in the game of life. Often the most earliest acquired milestone in life is the ability to not fear the thunder and tormented sounds of nature as a storm rattles the earth. It is simply nature. I was thrilled. There was seldom a time where rain like this didn't soak me to the core. It wasn't often that it rains here in this season. I was only until very recently a victim of rain, instead of able to appreciate it. Whenever a real rain storm rolled through at my old place, Larry and I would have to pack the window with plastic bags and tape to prevent the basement from flooding and soaking the place. It didn't happen often, but when it did we would not only be out of a place to sleep, but even being in the place was unbearable as the sound of the old sump pump in the basement was awful to be around. It was nice to not have that in my life anymore. I walk into the room again and look at myself in the mirror once more. I was going to get cleaned up. There was a small convenience store just next to the motel that sold disposable razors and groceries, so I decided I would go over and grab some things. I threw on my disgusting shoes and grabbed some money from the bag. I checked around for my keys and left the motel room in a hurry to try and get over to the store before the rain got too crazy. I checked to make sure the door was locked. Good to go. I scampered over to the store and walked in. There are a couple truckers conversing over by a quick pick lotto station. I walk over to the man working the counter and ask if they had any shaving razors and shampoo.

"Yup, over there, over behind the snacks and stuff. On the other side of the isle. The one that's facing the window. It's all over there."

"Okay cool, thank you very much." I say to him as I walk over to the goods.

It is like a little pharmacy over there. From nasal decongestant, to foot fungus spray. This little store has everything. I found some three pack packages of shaving razors and a little bottle of shaving cream. My beard was long so I grabbed two packs of the razors. This is going to be a hellish shaving experience using these little dual blade razors. There is a bit of personal sized shampoo bottles so I grab one of those as well. Q-tips? Yeah sure. That should be interesting. A little stick of deodorant. I fucking love capitalism. As I look up, I even see a little rack of souvenir t-shirts and stuff. I walk over to that. There is a dark blue shirt that had a picture of a big rig tractor trailer on it, and a couple flannel wool shirts. Both of those seem fine. After that I head over to the coolers and grabbed 2 bottles of water. My hands are officially full. It is strange to think I was going to actually be paying for this stuff as well.

I walk over to the counter and do my best to put the items down without dropping any. I realize I didn't have any food.

"Oh shit, I just gotta' grab one more thing. Be right back!" I say as I run over to the other side of the pharmacy section where some non perishable food was stored. I look it over pretty quickly and grab a can of beef ravioli and a package of freeze dried ramen noodles. I put those down on the counter as the attendant began scanning all the UPC codes on the items.

He says:

"Twenty-nine, ninety." as he bagged all the items in a plastic bag. I pulled two, $20 bills from my pocket and paid the man.
Damn, the fear that you get when you actually pay for something nice after stealing for so long is a rush. It almost felt like police are going to just show up and say something like "How bout' all this stuff!" as they lift up your shirt and a load of stolen goods fall out.

Not today though. These purchases are legit. That's right.

I thank the employee and walk out the door. Scampering quickly from the door of the convenience store over to the stairs and eventually the door of my motel room. I put the lock in the sticky door lock and jiggled the living hell out of it to try and get the rollers to catch and open the lock. After about 30 seconds it finally worked and I was free to put 100 lbs of pressure on the knob to try and get it to turn. It opened and I pushed the door open, walked in, and closed the door behind me. Forcing it shut, and locking it. I look around again, everything still in its right place. I began to head for the bathroom with the goods.
Shower first. The only way these razors stand a chance is if I do my best to clean the hell out of my beard and hair. So I ran the shower. The curtain was so old and crusty, it nearly kept its shape as I try to collapse it. I turned the knob and was greeted with roughly the same as the faucet. A long hiss of stale egg smelling air followed by some hard jolting pulses of water this time. Who knows the last time this shower was even used. After several minutes or so, the water was actually warm. It is my first warm shower in a comfortable place in maybe a year. As I drop my head in front of the stream of water a long stream of brown dirty water fell to the white basin of the shower. My skin felt oily and dank as the warm water penetrated through the grime of my greasy skin. It was so new. I grabbed the little bottle of shampoo that I had bought. I emptied about half the bottle into my hand and just lopped it right onto my head. I started

massaging the bubbles into my hair and beard. Weaving out tiny pebbles and other debris that found its way into the natty mess. Even as I rinsed it the first time, the mint green color of the shampoo was tainted with streaks of filth. I guess I should repeat. I dump the rest of the small bottle into my hand and the process repeats. This time with the rinse being much cleaner. I grab one of the free soaps that the motel was generous to provide and a hand cloth that I was going to improvise as a washcloth. As I did this, I remembered a trick to wash my pants, so I grabbed them off the floor and emptied the pockets and brought them into the shower with me.

    The trick is this, when you're broke long enough, you have to learn to clean yourself in interesting ways. Now, your clothes are no different, taking a shower is futile indeed if the clothes you wear after are just as dirty as you were. So the plan is to get the pants soaking wet and stand on them as I wash my body. This allows the left over soap running off my body to hopefully wash the pants the best it can. The weight of my body acting as an aggregator to squeeze out the filth tucked into the fibers. So this is exactly what I was doing. After that, it's just a matter of ringing out the jeans the best I can and letting them air dry. However, this motel bathroom had a hair dryer attached to the wall, so I was planning on using that to dry them.

    Before long, I was showered and feeling like a new man. The scruff on my face was feeling soft and more able to be shaved. So I proceed to do so. Applying the shaving cream and working it into the base of the some three inch mane that was hanging off my chin and neck. No more time to waste, I proceed to drag stroke after stroke in an attempt to remove the hair from my face. Making it only half way up one pass before feeling the razor grow noticeably duller and dragging on my skin. Luckily, I am very good at knowing the difference, as razor burn is an awful curse on mankind. Another slow, delicate pass and this particular razor is spent. So unpack another, and continue on mowing. Before long, and a whole mess of disposable razors later, my face is looking like a smooth piece of leather. Dotted with age marks and blackheads that were hiding beneath the bush. I went to town squeezing the filth from the pores. After all said and done, a cold splash of water was applied to ease the newly exposed skin. I grab the other hand towel off the bathroom banister and run it under cold water before applying it to my face.

    For the fist time in some time I am feeling naturally good. The drugs had all but worn off and left behind a newly appreciated love of what my mind had to offer. Naturally, I still craved some substance, but the appreciation for sobriety was palpable. I lay down on the hot mattress and mulled over what activity I could get into tonight. I put on the souvenir T-shirt and went about drying my pants in the bathroom.

    After several bouts of wringing and shaking, the pants are looking much cleaner and ready to be hit with the hair dryer. I could hear the heavy rain drops clapping on the roof of the motel over the sound of the noise of the hair dryer, which was for some reason comforting. As time went on, I could hear the heavy rain lift, and felt a new cool bit of air penetrate the walls and cracks of the room. A very relaxing atmosphere. The denim felt dry enough, so I shook them out once more and slid them on each leg.

I walk out the bathroom door and try to make a plan for what I could get into tonight. Perhaps a nice relaxing trip, or mellow opiate buzz from one of the pills in the bag. Then just kind of putter around the town and check out the water after the rain. The sun has gone down and the outside world seems quite mellow. I put on my shoes, tied them, and grabbed the back pack full of narcotics.

There was a prescription bottle in there that I had not yet dug into. It has some unmarked round pills in it, blue in color, and some other little yellow triangle ones. So I took one of each. I wasn't in the business of reconciling with my own mind. I had survived this far. What the hell is the worst that could happen? I grab a few hundred dollars from the cache and zip the bag up. Shoving it in a dresser drawer before heading towards the door. Exiting into the wild wet world of night time Smog Town.

I decide to head downtown, before making my way towards the water. The rain had turned to a cool night time mist that made the streetlights look very peculiar. A nestled hue that stuck around the light source, making the bright white LED bulbs seem almost yellow.

Conveniently enough, I walked about a quarter of a mile before a random taxi cab decided to pull up next to me and beep their horn. The driver, rolling down the passenger window before yelling over to me.

"Hey! You! You need a ride? Get you out of this rain?!"

I thought about it briefly and mumble to myself, "Yeah, why not."

I nod at the driver and headed over to the cab.

The cab is spotless. Honestly it must have been the cleanest cab in town. Which was impressive, but also alarming to some degree. He must not get a lot of patrons. Upon closing the door to the cab and getting in, the cabby says, in a very friendly way:

"Yeah, not to be rude. I just saw you walking in the rain and figured you could use a ride."

I am shocked by this type of friendly nature and in the most polite way possible, thanked the man.

"No it is fine man, I really appreciate it, to be honest."

"So where are ya' headed?" He asks.

I thought for a moment. Considering I had a bit more time before the drugs kicked in, and my body was still pretty beat up from the run in at Christina's grandmothers house. I guess a bar would do.

"Uh, well. I don't know. A bar downtown I guess."

"Any one in particular?" He asks.

"Not really, just nothing too expensive." I respond.

"Okay, gotcha'." He says, as putting the car into drive and pulling away from the curb.

The silence in the cab was growing a bit strange. It was one of those situations where you could tell that you would have a lot to talk about with this person. But the amount of allotted time was so brief that it would just be a forced dialogue of the common talking points. Of course, before I diverge into some crazy, drug fueled tangent that inevitably makes him so unconformable, that he kicks me from his cab.

A moment went by where I remedy myself of this thought. Not all people want to talk. Over time, it becomes almost a burden to remember all the faces, the names, the personality. Not to mention trying to keep a polite attitude with these people, all for the one moment where you say the wrong thing and screw it all up. Which I am quite good at.

By the time this thought passes, we are pulling up to the bar that the driver had chosen as suitable for me. A bar I was somewhat familiar with. This place called 'Gantry's' was a pretty small place with just a bar and a couple tables in it. Not bad.

"Alright, so not too long a ride. That will be seven sixty."

I pull the money out of my pocket. Hand the guy a twenty, and he breaks out change.

"Thanks again!" I say as I exit the cab and step onto the sidewalk.

"Not a problem, buddy. Just be careful out here." He says.

"Will do!" I respond.

The driver speeds off, and I walk towards the bar entrance. In the distance, down the street from where the bar was. I could see a group of three teenagers trying to use a wire hanger to try and bypass the locks on an old clunker. Oh, the magic of youth. I take a look at the bar before deciding to go talk to the hoodlums.

As I approach them, I can smell the skunk scented weed smoke that they are inhaling. As I got within about twenty-five feet of them, they took notice at my approach and quickly removed their makeshift door breaching device and hid the blunt they are smoking. Timid youngsters.

"It's okay y'all, I ain't the heat. Just seeing whats going on." I say.

They look at each other quite puzzled before one of them say:

"Okay? Well piss off old man before we fucking brain you."

I couldn't help but laugh at the threat, as these punks wouldn't last a day in my shoes. They would likely fail in jacking the car and go home to their parents house uptown and sleep off the shitty weed and aggression.

"Whoa whoa whoa! You got me all wrong gentlemen. Look, maybe I can be of some help to y'all. Or, of course, maybe you want to take a little more time doing that, which gives old Officer Dingus up the way just a little bit more time to drive by and bust y'all."

These adolescent trouble makers had no experience, nor had they ever likely had to try to open your car door with a hanger or length of string because you locked your keys in the car after drinking too much. Never the less, they are taken back by my forward approach to danger.

"Alright old man. Let's see what you got than." The alpha punk says.

Wow, they keep calling me old man. Jeez, the years must have been rough. Never matter, I walked briskly over to the car. I see that they are trying to wedge the door with some old paint stirrers and use a wire hanger to get between the door skin and door handle to pop the door open from the inside. A factory safety feature that surely was not well thought out. So I start looking around the interior of the car, and don't see any indication of there being an active car alarm. So I took the lead.

"Alright, one of you, give me your shoe lace." I say.

They look at each other quite puzzled and one of them says:

"What the fuck for? What the hell are you gonna do with a shoe lace dumb ass."

These kids are funny. Only one of them was actually wearing traditional shoes. The other two are in flip-flops. I look at them briefly, as a car starts heading up the block.

"Shit! Get down!" I say.

I drop to the ground as the three boys just stand there, all murmuring "what the fuck?"
They really didn't give a shit about what they are doing. So to hell with it. I lifted my self off the ground, wiped a leaf off my shirt and quickly apologized.

"Anyway, yeah, give me your shoelace, come on, chop chop!"

The alpha punk gives a look at the shoe wearing punk and just reluctantly nods as to just get it over with. The shoe bearing teenager very woefully removes his beat up old shoe and begins taking the lace out of the eyelets while saying:

"Bullshit ass grandpa shit, this better work or else I am gonna' beat your ass."

I laugh a little before saying:

"Well, okay tough guy. We can grab ass later. For now why don't you just gimme' the string and keep the bullshit to a minimum."

He pull the lace through the last eyelet and hands it over.

"Awesome." I say, as I tied a lassoing knot into the middle of the lace.
"Alright, we are in business. Now pay attention children, you might learn something."

I remember watching Larry try to break into some old car a while ago and went about this method he said his dad taught him when he was a kid.

"See, all you gotta do, is be smarter than the lock." I say, as I slid one end of the string through the gap they had created with the makeshift paint stirrer shims.

"Hand me the wire?" I ask.

I take the wire and bend a little hook on the end of it to help grab the end of the string that is dangling inside the car. Once I get a grip on it, I pull it diagonally, underneath their shims, and pull it out the door jam side of the door.

"Alright, perfect!" I say as I grab the other end of the string with my right hand.

"Now, It's just a matter of getting that little loop around the door lock pin, or the handle, I will go for the pin."

The hoodlums look on amazed by the idea.

I started wiggling the string down gently and positioned it on top of the vertical door lock pin. Moving it slightly before the lasso fell perfectly on top of the little rod. As I applied a little bit of tension to the ends of the string, it tightened the lasso around the rod, allowing me to simply lift the string ends, and…

'Pop.'
The door unlocks.

"Yahtzee." I say.

"Holy shit!" The punks say as they begin to scurry and push me out of the way so they can rip the car door open.

"Alright boys, here is your shoelace, dude." The shoe bearing punk thanks me as he grabs the shoe lace and dives head first into the festivities. The punks start tearing into the car and ripping the glove box open and rummaging through it. I look on, somewhat proud of my work. My work is done, time to head back to the bar.

Cars began passing by the bar, illuminating the punks rummaging through the car. It was as I landed my foot on the front steps of the bar that I heard a door slam nearby. I opened the door to the bar as a chime of aggravated yelling ensued towards the boys.

Shortly after, several gun shots rang out. As I entered the bar, all the patrons rushed out the open door to see what was going on. Cleared the bar right out. So I sat at the corner spot. The bartender, who is hanging about 75% of his body over the end of the bar to get a glimpse out the window to see what was going on, politely greeted me with an:

"Oh shit, here we go again."

I couldn't care less what was going on out there. Not like in a reckless way, But I think the pills are starting to take control. So all I could say is:

"Hey can I get a drink?"

The bartender looks at me. A subtle humor mixed with shocked expression on his face. He sighed and says, "yeah, just hold on" as he falls back into the bar and grabs the phone. I hear him dial 9-1-1 as his face turned somewhat ghostly white. I heard him speak as he went into the back room and stutter a little as he spoke to the responder.

"I- I think I just witnessed a murder."

Holy shit, was this for real? I turn around in my chair and look over at the car I just helped the punks break into. Two of them, the two wearing flip-flops, were lying in the street, blood pouring from ones chest and head and the other, roughly the same. The third, who was kind enough to lend me the shoelace, was inside the car and even at this distance, I could see the specs of blood and flesh on the rear window and cloth interior. I sunk into my chair as I feel a strong feeling of self disgust fall over me. This is bad.

"Hey bartender. How bout' that drink?"

He just looks at me as he hung up the phone.

"Uh, yeah.. Sure. What will it be?" He says, visibly trying to remain calm and just comprehend what the hell was going on.

"Cool, well. I don't know. Let me get a triple of Makers Mark?" I say.

The bartender grabs a glass from under the bar and says, "rocks?"

"Nah, just straight up."

He pours the drink, and as soon as he tilts the bottle back upright to finish pouring I snatch the glass and suck back half of its contents. He turns around to put the bottle back, but by that time I had already finished the glass.

"Hold up! Let me do another, and then I will cash out if that is okay."

The bartender smirks a little as he returns to fill the glass again.

"Thanks, man."

This one I enjoy a bit slower, but the ever present thought that sooner than later, police are going to be showing up here and will be asking a hell of a lot of questions. Best not be around for that. Last thing I want is to give a statement to police, half in the bag, and zooming on random pills that I keep in a pink backpack at the hotel I am currently living at, funded all with ill gotten gains. Living on the street is shitty, but a hell of a lot better than a cage.

People slowly started to re enter the bar. Quietly I should say. You could hear a pin drop over their silence. Most of them, just as pale as the bartender. One of the patrons sat down next to me and just put his hands on the bar and put his head down. I heard him say:

"Oh my god. What the fuck."

I was taken back by this so I pause for a second and ask him:

"What's up man, are you okay?"

He looks up at me quickly before putting his head down again and with hesitation he says:

"Ye- Yeah.. I'm alright. I just saw someone get shot in the face but I think I am alright."

I am speechless. I mean, what do you say to a guy after he saw something like that. He lifted his head and proceeds to ask me a question.

"Hey, not to sound like an idiot, but like, this is real life right? Like you are here right now?"

I laugh a little.

"Uh, yeah. I think so man. I guess if you mean, did I just see what you saw, yes. And if you are really sitting here next to me, yes. This is real life bud."

He looks at me, nods slightly and sinks slowly back into his own arms. Damn, talk about a fragile mind. I hear loads of stories about soldiers and gang members, all having terrible bouts of post traumatic stress after witnessing killings and what not. Which makes a load of sense to me. If I wasn't almost directly responsible, and a fucking drug addict, I would likely be melting deeper into my own arms than this poor guy was already melted into his. At this point the bartender returned with my tab, eighteen dollars and thirty cents. I thank the man and casually put a twenty dollar bill on the counter. I can hear sirens in the distance so I just throw back the drink, give a deep exhale to relieve the burn, and stand up slowly.

My heart starts to pound. I could feel it in my neck and head. But it shortly after subsided. So I went about leaving. While passing, I give the guy next to me a pat on the back and say quietly to him:

"It'll be okay, man. Just breath, okay?"

As I left the bar, which was silent except for the rerun hockey game that was playing on the bar's flat screen TV. I thank the bartender casually and walked down the steps, letting the door close on its own behind me.

I could see several people still gathered outside the scene onlooking as the cops arrive. The car owner in his underwear and a wife beater, standing outside his apartment with the gun resting on the porch behind him. People are on their cell phones calling whoever, likely friends, loved ones, or police. The red and blue flashing lights are flooding the road while the yellow flashing of the ambulance is going in and out of synchronicity with the police lights. It is almost rhythmic and calming. Either way, I am out of there and looking as little as possible at the hell on earth that just happened. I start to walk, and could certainly feel the liquor begin to mix with what subtle effect that the pills are having. It feels quite foreign to me. A feeling of tightness, yet loose. Almost like a dehydrated vasoconstriction feeling mixed with a carefree ecstasy that felt somewhat warm. A feeling that the buffoonery hidden in the alcohol was surely to perpetuate. A nervous smirk came across my face as I try to get away from the turmoil behind me. I am starting to really sympathize with that random guy at the bar. This was absolutely insane to witness. Short of heading back to the hotel and getting even more twisted off of whatever was available in the cache of narcotics, I feel that I need to just wander. The town is somewhat alive tonight. Even though it was a piss smelling rainy night, people seem to be out and about and in decent spirits. Which is inspiring in a way, because it gave me some sort of confirmation that I was on the right path. Maybe my choices going forward tonight, could be fueled with some sort of positive energy in the air. I head the only direction that made any sense to go to, and that was the beach, to watch the tide roll in after the storm.

My mind is getting flooded with mixed emotions. Fueled by quick snip flashbacks to times in my life when things were better, or far worse. Love once felt. Hatred in retrospect. It all was pouring in like the buckets of rain that cleansed the dirty streets of this town. The light's of the cars passing by acting as bursts of light to begin and end new checkpoints of memories in my head. My mind is surely a grand spectacle, and my eyes, the humble observers. Paying their way in blood for the ticket to view it. I felt calm. Calmer than I should have been. My legs were essentially on autopilot as the little man inside of me pulled the levers to make them work.

"Where is she." I whisper. A memory of the woman I miss so much begins to make my vision a little more wet with sadness.

Her smile, glowing like the warm sunset's that we shared with each other, and all those times on the beach. The curves of her body mixing with my physique in an intimate tangle of majestic splendor. Like a pair of phoenixes making passionate love as they fall to the earth. One, flying away before the other smacks the hard concrete. I remember her embrace. The power it had over me. I could feel it now, as real as the burning that was plaguing my sinuses as the emotion began to take control of my tears and moral compass. I wouldn't be who I am without her. I wouldn't be a shred of the success, or a lanyard of the failure that I am, without the pain and pleasure that the yin to my yang let me be. She was it. She was my love, and these are all the memories I wanted to forget.

Prior to my affluent and ever present failure of a life that this thought made me understand for the millionth time. It made me realize that it was me. It is my fault. All of it. If I just cared a little more. If I just stopped and smelled the fucking flowers once in a while, my life wouldn't be a flaming pile of dog shit on the step of mankind. There was no grand parade for my demise. No honorable mention. No valor in my embrace. I made my own failures, and it has taken me to now to finally realize it. I might as well of just laid down in the damn street at this point. Let the passing memories just run me over and end this charade once and for all.

That is when fight or flight kicks in, or maybe the drugs. You can't just give up. I can't just let this have me. Not after all the shit I have been through. It's not fair. But is this just that same destructive ego talking? Probably.

Remember, I am but a humble nail. My mind? The hammer. Nailing the nail into a rotted board that is the destroyed frame and foundation that is my life.

Unashamed of my tears, I walk on. I have water to see. I could swear I see myself drive by in the shadows from the passing lights. While I gaze on from the curb, a bright red convertible, clearly in contrast from the hue of the surrounding night life. A handsome man, driving it with the top down, in hardly appropriate weather. Even the radio chatter rang a bell as I winced my eyes to try and see it pass, but it was gone in a quick glimpse.

That one hurt. Remembering that day. That fucking day. That day was everything, and my fragile mind must have just broken as it became reminiscent. Why did I ever leave her?

I can still hear her sobering plea:
"Stay with me, Bruce! There is nowhere else to be! Just stay, watch the sunset with me like we planned!"

The warm orange sun falling on her skin. As I took this sweet moment for granted. Why the fuck wouldn't I just stay there. Instead I left that moment forever. Finding it presumably much more important to be where ever the hell I was going that day. Driving with the top down and listening to music.

Where the hell was I going that day? I remember it was very important to me.

It hit me like a stone…

Jerry.

I was going to that fucking hole in the wall store to pick up that piece of merchandise that Jerry had. Who Jerry was, is not as important as what ever he sold me that day. I was so obsessed with that piece.
A glass figure that dated back like 500 years. Supposedly some amazing relic that brings fortune to whoever holds it. It should have been a damn wedding ring. How could I be so fucking stupid? I ditched the only women who would ever love me to meet with a back alley merchant to buy some rarity of a useless mineral, that I felt was more important or valuable than the real gem, that I had in front of me.

I could hardly walk anymore. Knowing how stupid I am is making me sick to my stomach. I don't even know what the hell happen to that stupid relic. I think I slapped it in the trunk of the car and just forgot about it. A true sign of just how ignorant I was in my own glory. How unbelievably stupid.

My goodness it is such a common theme. All the people who care about me, all the love I had. Let alone with the opposite sex. Even just having Larry around, I clearly took for granted. Now look at me. A polished turd, feeling his way down a narrow curb, in a smelly part of town.

Nobody here to heed my sorrow, no one to give me quarter. Just a sad sack of shit with an uneven shave. There is no drug in the world that would ever change that. Not even I can change that. I am feeling it. What else is there to do. When you are this low, even something at sea level seems like it is on a tower made of ivory. The irony.

I can smell the salt water blowing towards the inside of the town. A slight light in the tunnel of my own mind that snapped me back into motion to just get to the water.

It is now a mission, instead of a choice. Wandering like a lost dog. Guided by my last working sense, the scent of the ocean. It holds strange relevance to me at this point. The tides, they come in, and they move out. Cleaning the filth from the shores and dragging it into the deep, where it is forgotten. Of course, until a third party attempts to find it, either by chance or on purpose.

      Inland is not safe from its wrath either. The water heats up, floats into the atmosphere where it condenses and falls back to the dirty ground. Cleaning, and filtering itself in the process. This mess, that us people create, often settling back on top of us as we think it is being wisped away. When really, we are but a mark of time for where the water is really moving to.

      My urgency to see the water is only getting fueled by the number of passing cars heading away from the beach. As they knew that the tide heading out meant that the show was over. It was only a matter of time before the shores turned from a somber coast line, into a smelly cesspool of all their filth and shame. I care not. This is my witching hour, and I need it's beauty.

      Before long, I arrive at the entrance to the park that bordered the coast. The lights emanating their orange yellow warmth look much like little suns to me. The rain around them making a slight rainbow effect, that either due to the drugs or the perception, hurt my eyes to look at. I am not afraid to be here this time. I have forgot all about what had happened here just a few days ago. I could even still see the remnants of the caution tape that the police had left following the incident that happened. All tattered and ripped and blowing in the coastal breeze.

      I finally feel at ease.

      I slow down my pace and all the pain and torture my mind was putting me through stopped. For a moment, I felt warm. Never mind the damp awful weather that is running right through me, and the cocktail of pharmaceuticals that are romping through my bloodstream.

      It makes me smile. A dizzying, psychopathic smile. However short lived by a pain that walking had made my body feel. My joints feel weak, my muscles burn and I know that it is about time I find a place to sit and relax.

      I walk a short while longer before finding a nice rock wall to rest on. The rocks border the water in a way that let me sprawl out a bit and catch my breath, as the pills are really sapping me of my energy. Sitting down has a feeling similar of how a tremendous pile of shit must feel when it is squeezed onto the dirt of the local playground. A truly unwelcome, yet relieving energy to it all.

      It began to feel like work to keep my head up, and my eyes open. But this is work worth doing.

      I decide to lay on my side, propping myself up by my elbow and allowing my body and legs to relax as I overlook the water. My heart somewhat pounding from the walk, appreciating the quick relief. Things start to plague my mind. The hotel room, the backpack, the money. That was all eerily easy to vanquish however. None of it mattered, and if it did, I wouldn't be here. I wouldn't be sitting here. A dirty pile of shit, high on unknown pills, looking into the water for answers to problems that I made for myself.

The answer was always me. I was just too stupid to realize that. See, it doesn't matter who you think you are or who you might actually be. If you don't stop and feel the curb sometimes, it will hit you like a ton of bricks.

"Oh, fuck! Ouch!"

My chest begins to hurt. Not in an unfamiliar way, but it isn't entirely welcome either. Years of drug abuse and living off of stolen candy bars, smoking makeshift cigarettes sometimes causes these types of issues.

The pain quickly went away, as I feel a cold pain rush to the arm I am laying on, and bringing with it a warm relaxing feeling of dizziness, not unlike a good buzz. A feeling I know all too well. A feeling so nice, it gave me chills. There is no more rain. No more fear of the dark, nothing. I am just here. Forever. I could hear the hollow clapping of footsteps on the ground behind me as the feeling of peace dragged my eyes closed, and off to sleep. I don't deserve to feel this good. I deserve to feel cold, alone, and scared.

The footsteps seem to turn away with this thought, and walk further away. This makes me feel scared, but brought with it the peace I actually deserved. It was time to sleep, and nothing could interrupt me this time.

* *

There he sat, pondering his next move, as if he had one. The way the world was turning had its effect on him and he fell off. Falling gently to the waters edge, where the rain and tides of the water pulled him into the abyss. His soul in retrograde.

Forever feeling the curb.

The End.

www.ingramcontent.com/pod-product-compliance
Lightning Source LLC
LaVergne TN
LVHW011840060526
838200LV00054B/4110